KEVIN
THANKS FOR EV

SIN CITY RETRIBUTION

A GAME CALLED REVENGE

RICK HART

SIN CITY RETRIBUTION: A GAME CALLED REVENGE

1405 SW 6th Avenue • Ocala, Florida 34471 • Phone 352-622-1825 • Fax 352-622-1875
Website: www.atlantic-pub.com • Email: sales@atlantic-pub.com
SAN Number: 268-1250

Library of Congress Cataloging-in-Publication Data

Names: Hart, Rick, 1948- author.
Title: A game called revenge / by Rick Hart.
Description: Ocala, Florida : Atlantic Publishing Group, Inc., 2020. |
Series: Sin City retribution; 2 | Summary: "Turk continues his quest for retribution after his prized motorcycle is stolen"— Provided by publisher.
Identifiers: LCCN 2019045995 (print) | LCCN 2019045996 (ebook) | ISBN 9781620236949 (paperback) | ISBN 162023694X (paperback) | ISBN 9781620236956 (ebook)
Classification: LCC PS3608.A7867 G36 2020 (print) | LCC PS3608.A7867 (ebook) | DDC 813/.6—dc23
LC record available at https://lccn.loc.gov/2019045995
LC ebook record available at https://lccn.loc.gov/2019045996

Printed in the United States

PROJECT MANAGER: Katie Cline
INTERIOR LAYOUT AND JACKET DESIGN: Nicole Sturk

TABLE OF CONTENTS

1972

CHAPTER I

THE JOURNEY BEGINS

Nevada has and always will be a badass state. It is the wild, wild west so to speak. You could easily die here— at the hands of an outlaw mobster, from your own stupidity, or both— and end up being dinner for the buzzards, never to be heard from again. Yes, this is where I call home.

Everyone knew that Las Vegas was run by the mob in the '70s, and the desert was full of the scavenger-picked, sun-dried bones of fools who had dared to take them on. The funny thing is, it didn't scare the locals. In fact, it actually made them feel safer. Nobody shit on Vegas without getting dumped on harder, and that was the Noblemen's philosophy too.

With a riding season that lasted all year, my brothers and I tore through the harsh Nevada desert, howling with passion for the wind in our faces and the vibration of the steel between our legs. The roar of over 20 Harleys would slice through the desert heat and vibrate into our very souls. We rode like there was no tomorrow and partied just as fast.

It may be hard for outsiders to understand, but the club patch held us together. It represented the brotherhood we shared. And that brotherhood gave most of us something to believe in when society had let us down.

We had just rolled out of the '60s into the '70s without much change in our outlook on life.

As the saying goes, if it ain't broke, don't fix it. And while others might have looked down on us, there was nothing about the Noblemen that needed fixing. Our little subculture of unique individuals made up the soul of our club and gave each member strength.

But you didn't just 'join' a society as tightly banded as ours. Becoming a part of our club came in levels. First, you became a friend of the club's. You could attend certain parties and runs, but a vast majority of activity was off-limits. Then, after a while, you moved up to the status of 'hang-around.' At that point, the club starts to take a serious look at you and gets an idea of what your intentions are. And by then, your riding skills better be up to par, or it's a no-go. Joining up alongside a group of hell-raising, hardcore bikers isn't like a nice Sunday drive—it requires some serious skill. Once you get to the point of being a 'hang-around,' you meet all the members, so they can figure out who you really are; they need to know if you're the kind of guy who can be their brother.

Then, when you finally make prospect, it is because a member stood up for you and said he would be your sponsor. And you better be ready to wear the bottom rocker because it carries a lot of responsibility and will change your life. As a prospect, the club will be watching to see what you're made of and how badly you want to be a full-patched member.

Hiney went on to become my sponsor, and he took me under his wing right away. I was proud to wear that bottom rocker. I had a lot to learn and prove to the club. It took me some time to fully understand everything about how the club functioned, and it was an up and down road. The trials were numerous and thought-provoking. Every situation was a test—anything from picking up a package that didn't exist to a mock confrontation between a civilian and a member to see if you would step in.

As a prospect with the Noblemen, I either went without sleep or was just plain afraid to close my eyes. I never knew what to expect from minute to minute. It seemed like every day I was facing new trials I had never come up against before. I didn't want my life with the club to be a series of hits and misses.

When the shit got deep, I found myself on top of my Harley, pipes blasting so loud that it'd drown out the evil thoughts I had for the people who insisted on testing my abilities and loyalty. I knew the road to full patch would carry a heavy price, but it was a struggle at times to be disrespected by members who would push you beyond your limits, then yell at you when you failed. It was an everyday beat down, but I wasn't alone. I saw the other prospects taking the same abuse, so I knew it wasn't personal. And I knew the prize would be so sweet in the end.

The club served up its own justice. It was always cut and dry—no bullshit. The members knew who they could trust, who would always be there when you needed them. The patch holders lived their lives knowing that a handshake was good enough amongst themselves. As I prospected, I learned that every member had a purpose and something to bring to the table—and that's why they tested us so hard.

Meeting Hiney was a turning point in my life. Since that eventful day in a dingy Vegas bar, the scene had run though my mind a hundred times. That was the day everything changed.

That was the day I remember saying…as I grinned confidently…, "What do I want? I want to join up with you guys."

"Is that a fact?" Stroker sneered, tossing his rubber mallet aside. "Do you even have a clue what we're about?"

"If it has anything to do with Harleys, girls, and fighting, I'm in."

There was a beat of silence before Stroker cracked a smile. He laughed and shook my hand boisterously.

"I respect that. There's a come-around period. You have to show us you're serious. If we like you and you still like us, you become a hang-around. You'll hang with us, come to our parties, and get to know what'll be expected of you. At that point, if we decide to seriously consider letting you become a member, we'll make you a club prospect." His smile became a little more wicked. "We'll find your breaking point and cross it a hundred times over. We gotta be sure you really want it. Still interested?" He raised an eyebrow inquisitively.

"Phew!" I pushed my breath through pursed lips. "Sounds like you're going to run my ass into the ground…When do I start?"

With a nod, Stroker said, "Hiney is your sponsor. If you fuck up, we kick both your asses," he said mostly at Hiney. "So," Stroker turned to face me again. "What do we call you?"

"Hey man, I'm just the turkey who saved Hiney's ass. Call me whatever you want." I was just being a smartass, but the name stuck.

"All right, Turkey," Stroker said, clapping his hands together and rubbing them in anticipation. "Let's get you started." Glancing at the engine he'd been working on, he said, "Go grab that Linkert carb off the table and start bolting it to that mill."

Thank God I had taken an auto-mechanics class in high school. I had just enough knowledge to fake me through the installation. I bolted it on but left the fine-tuning to Stroker. We drank and talked well into the night. I made some very good friends that day and learned quite a bit about Linkerts.

The club dominates you while you're a prospect, as I soon learned. Until we were full-patched, we were not allowed to sit in on the meetings. Prospects stood outside for hours until the meeting was over, acting as lookouts. It didn't matter if it was 100° or 0°, raining or shining—we stood our post no matter what.

I was outside one evening with four other prospects. We were shooting the shit and getting to know one another when Doc stepped out into the garage.

"Prospects, get your asses over here."

We all ran over to the garage immediately, as if we were dogs being whistled to by our master. With an angry glint in his eye, Doc looked each of us over.

"Who here likes to fight?"

I didn't know if it was a trick question or not, but I raised my hand nevertheless. Everyone else remained silent.

"That would be me. I love to fight."

I hoped I wasn't being stupid by opening my mouth, but my hesitancy vanished when Doc said, "Only one of you prospects likes to fight?" He made a disgusted noise and continued. "Well, you four cowards take a hike. Come see me if you ever grow some balls."

A stunned silence followed, but no one moved.

"Did you hear me, motherfuckers?! Get out of my sight before I show you how much a real Nobleman likes to fight!"

The four rejected prospects turned and headed out of the garage. As the sound of their bikes skidding out onto the highway reached where we stood, Doc turned to me and said, "What are you looking at, tough guy? Get back out in the yard and keep an eye on our bikes."

"You got it, man."

I left the garage and resumed my position alone in the front yard. As simple as it may have been, I had passed the first test, and I felt damn good about that. I wasn't exaggerating either. I loved to fight. When things got tough, I didn't hesitate to crack heads. That was what I trained hard to do in the dojo. I was a dedicated martial artist, and I trained at least three days a week. I was a black belt in Tae Kwon Do, and I didn't have a problem proving it. I quickly got a name for myself with the club as a fighter. The members liked that and preferred to have me inside with them, leaving the other prospects outside with the bikes.

I liked being inside with the patch-holders, and Baby Huey kept me close while he was drinking. Anyone who wanted to talk to Baby Huey had to go through me first. Prospects were not allowed to drink while out with the club, but Huey sometimes made an exception for me. He'd tell me to go get a couple of shots and then make me do one of them. It pissed off the other prospects, but I didn't care. I knew where I stood with the club, and I wanted that full patch on my back.

Everywhere I went, I kept my ears open for info about my stolen bike, but it didn't take long for me to decide that these guys weren't the thieves. I figured I still might hear something from someone who knew about it, but after a while, it started to fade from my mind. My attention became consumed with becoming a full-patched member. Nothing was going to interfere with that—not even my retribution.

The club was becoming my life. I had made some strong friendships in the club, and the camaraderie had become something I didn't want to lose. I was slowly getting to know all the members in the club and getting real tight with the club procedures. As in all walks of life, there were a few members that I just didn't care for, but on the whole, most of them became family to me.

Baby Huey, a former Vietnam combat veteran who'd served two tours, was the club president. He was a tower of a man who demanded respect, controlling the club like a drill sergeant. I liked his attitude.

Doc was the club's vice president. He sat quietly and basically let Huey run the show, but you didn't want to set him off. He had his own way of doing things, and when Huey wasn't around, no one defied his orders.

Stroker was the clubs Sergeant at Arms, and he had a very short fuse. He would rather hit you upside the head than talk to you. He was a hulking guy and intimidated everyone. Baby Huey seemed to be the only one who could tame his temper. But you had to love Stroker for who he was. Most members avoided him, but I made it my mission to get in tight with him.

And, of course, Hiney and I became good friends. He was a very likeable guy, but I personally thought he was too friendly with people outside the club. He owned a red 1952 Harley Panhead. I begged him to let me ride it even after he told me that it had a suicide clutch. No one wants to ride a bike with a suicide clutch, but I was eager to learn, so we switched bikes on occasion. I had a blast driving that rigid-framed panhead around town.

Every club member had a different personality, but they were all here for one purpose—the brotherhood. The Noblemen allowed you to be yourself, and with such a mixed bag, not everyone in the club got along. There were times when this caused internal problems, but they were swiftly dealt with by the Sergeant at Arms. But no matter what little quarrels were happening internally, the Noblemen were brothers who stood together against other clubs and citizens. It was that kinship that attracted me to them.

One Saturday morning, the club made a run to Red Rock Canyon. From my position at the back of the pack with the other prospects, I was mesmerized by the thunder from dozens of iron horses echoing off of the desert rock walls. It sounded like a roar from some otherworldly beast—a long, monotonous bellow rather than 20 individual drones.

I found out early that when you ride hard with a bunch of guys who would literally die for each other, the fear of cops, other gangs, or the general public disappeared. It was like your senses heightened when you rode with the gang—you were always aware of your environment and the people around you. It just happened naturally. You were never afraid of what could happen, but you always prepared for the worst. It's just how our minds worked. There was no single man within the Noblemen—it was all for one, one for all. If an outsider challenged one of us, he soon learned that he'd threatened the whole club. And that was a lesson no one soon forgot.

We slowly rode through Red Rock and headed straight for Bonnie Springs Bar. As we approached, the pack slowed down, which was a signal for the prospects to break ranks and speed ahead to the bar to check it out. The members always wanted to know what the scene looked like at the bar before they arrived. No one wanted to ride blindly into a hornet's nest, so we were the scouts.

Shorty and I had volunteered before the club had set out, so we cut rank and sped past the pack. We had to bust our asses to get there with enough time to properly scout out the situation before the rest of the guys rolled up.

We weren't surprised to see about a dozen other Harleys out front when we arrived at Bonnie Springs Bar; it was a popular place for bikers. Still, I motioned for Shorty to head back and inform the club while I stuck around to find out a bit more about our bar-mates. I backed my bike in right in line with the others, and as soon as I climbed off my scoot, I was approached by three prospects from the other club.

"Who the fuck are you?" a barrel-chested prospect asked me.

Ignoring his question and jumping straight to the point, I responded, "Look, fellas. We can be friends or enemies. I don't really care which. How about you pick one."

The motley crew pushed in, trying to intimidate me. I took a short step away from my bike to make more room to move in case it came to a fight.

"Don't be a smart-ass with me!" yelled the lankier of the bunch. "I'm no punk."

"Hey man," I said, throwing up my hands innocently. "I didn't mean any disrespect. Who are you guys with?"

"We're with the Mad Dogs," the barrel-chested guy growled in what he must have thought was a menacing way. "Who are *you* with?"

I smiled as the roar of 20 approaching Harleys answered his question.

"I guess you'll find out soon enough."

Baby Huey had the pack back their bikes into an area separated from the Mad Dogs' Harleys. While it'd be perfectly easy to just pull into a spot and shut off the engine, the Noblemen always backed their bikes up against a building in the direction of the exit. That way police couldn't easily read our rear license plate numbers before we noticed them scouting us out. It also gave us the opportunity for quick get-aways, which we often needed.

The cacophony hadn't gone unnoticed, and by the time the guys were walking up to me, the whole porch was full of growling Mad Dogs. Baby Huey, Doc, and Stroker strode straight up to the Mad Dog officers. The conversation started off calmly enough; Huey wasn't one to start shit for no reason. But it didn't take long for it to become apparent that we weren't welcome.

"Well," Huey said, his voicing raising in frustration, "I assure you we aren't leaving. So, I guess it's your move." His shoulders were stiffening in what I'd come to find out was a tell-tale sign of him preparing for a fight.

To give credit where it's due, one of the Mad Dog officers seemed to be more level-headed than the rest of the bunch. "Hey man, you don't see us riding up on your hangouts. You should show us the same respect."

"You know what, we would if we respected you," Huey said tersely. "But tell you what, since this is neither of our territories, we'll share the bar with you. But your guys will need to sit in the back by the duck pond."

Another Mad Dog officer shouted, "Fuck you man! Where do you get off thinking you can tell us—"

"Are you going to stand there talking or are you going to do something about it?" Huey cut in, stepping into the pup's face and staring him down.

After a beat of silence, one of the Mad Dog officers jumped on Baby Huey's back, and it was on!

The fight spilled out into the parking lot as the Mad Dogs jumped off the porch to meet us head on. I tried to make it over to Huey, who had three guys on him, but I was stopped by on oncoming body who seemed intent on taking my head off. I let him swing at me, dodged it, and then my elbow connected with his jaw. I kicked his leg out from under him, and his body went up in the air and came down hard. I heard the air rush out of him like a loose balloon. I was confident he wasn't getting up anytime soon, so I turned to face my next opponent.

We outnumbered them by a few guys, which made it hard to find someone to hit who wasn't already fighting, but I managed. These guys wanted to make a name for themselves by trying to take us on, but they underestimated us. We were sure to show them why we were the ones who deserved respect.

I got to Huey just in time to see him throw the last Mad Dog to the ground. He walked over to the Mad Dog president, who was crouched and trying to stop the blood flow from the top of his head, and said, "On second thought, you guys go ahead and keep the duck pond. We're out of here."

"Fuck you, man. This ain't over!" the president spat.

Huey reached down and grabbed a handful of the Dog's blood-drenched hair, pulling his face up to meet his.

"Did I say it was over, motherfucker?" Huey yelled as red spittle flew from his mouth. "Next time I see a Mad Dog patch in Vegas, it's war. You hear me? War!"

Baby Huey slammed the Mad Dog's head into the nearby wall with a sickening crunch. He threw his arm over Stroker's shoulder as he hopped off the porch and headed back towards the bikes.

As the Mad Dogs stumbled about, trying to regain their bearings, Huey shouted, "Let's get the fuck out of here. We'll let the cops clean this mess up."

Our bikes roared to life, louder than I have ever heard them before. We sped through the dirt parking lot, sending rocks and sand flying, leaving the Mad Dogs in our dust—literally. We hit the main road and turned towards Blue Diamond, figuring the cops would be responding up Charleston from the other direction.

Speeding down Blue Diamond road, we made a left onto Rainbow Boulevard, a two-lane asphalt road that ran from Blue Diamond Road to Fremont Street. It was a lousy, unkept road full of dips and potholes, but we'd be more likely to avoid contact with the responding police if we took it.

My heart was racing as we flew down Rainbow Boulevard with the sound of sirens fading behind us. I was so excited. I couldn't believe we'd taken on another club, and I had gotten to be a part of it. I couldn't get the smile off my face. That was the coolest thing I had ever done, and I was hooked. I decided then and there that I wanted to make this club my life.

CHAPTER 2

THE BACK STREET TAVERN

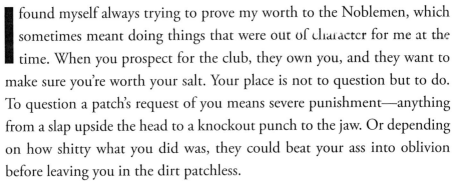

I found myself always trying to prove my worth to the Noblemen, which sometimes meant doing things that were out of character for me at the time. When you prospect for the club, they own you, and they want to make sure you're worth your salt. Your place is not to question but to do. To question a patch's request of you means severe punishment—anything from a slap upside the head to a knockout punch to the jaw. Or depending on how shitty what you did was, they could beat your ass into oblivion before leaving you in the dirt patchless.

Hiney was my sponsor while I prospected for the club, so I was under his wing and his command. Most of the patches ignored me like they did the other prospects, but there were always some who loved to torment us. Hiney and I had been friends since day one, and he treated me with respect. He inadvertently shielded me from the wrath of other patches but not without some cost to himself.

One night, Hiney and I were putting down a few beers and shooting the breeze behind the clubhouse one Friday night when Baron walked out.

"What the fuck do you think you're doing, Prospect?" he yelled.

I took another sip of beer and said mildly, "Just kicking back with my sponsor. What can I do for you, Baron?"

"Well for starters, you need to get out front and clean my scoot. And hand me that beer you're drinking, it's mine now."

Baron reached out for my beer but was stopped by Hiney as he stepped between us.

"Back off, Baron," he said. "The prospect is doing my bidding now."

"That's bullshit, man!" Baron yelled, stepping into Hiney's face. "What's wrong, Hiney? Can't you get any of the other members to drink with you? Is that why you're drinking out back here with the prospect? Pretty pathetic."

"I choose the company I keep, and no one's going to tell me I can't." Hiney closed the small gap between them, bringing himself nose to nose with Baron. An evil smile crossed Baron's face—he was enjoying every second of this. Without moving his face an inch, Baron's eyes turned and focused on me.

"Why are you still here, Prospect? I thought I told you to get out front."

Baron held his hand out and made a "give it" gesture toward my beer. I handed my beer to Baron, who snatched it and, with a triumphant smile, chugged the last bit of it.

"Baron," Hiney yelled, "I've had enough of your—"

"Hiney," I interrupted him. "It's cool." The last thing I wanted to do was make any enemies in the club. Even one or two bad votes could keep you out of the club, and this wasn't worth that risk. I figured Baron was just doing his job to see how much shit I was willing to put up with to get voted in. I was determined to get my full patch, no matter what it took.

Hiney was giving me a look that told me I had fucked up, but I just turned and walked inside the clubhouse. I stood in the dining room for a moment, hoping I had made the correct decision without making Hiney look bad.

"That's right, Prospect!" Baron shouted from outside. "I want my bike to shine."

I was looking under the sink to see if I could find some rags and cleaner for Baron's bike when the back door swung open and then slammed shut. Still down on one knee, I looked over my left shoulder to see Hiney standing over me with his hands balled in tight fists.

"When I tell you to stay seated, you damn well better stay seated, asshole. You just made me look stupid in front of Baron."

I stood up with the rags and a bottle of cleaner in my arms and turned to face Hiney.

I tried to keep my voice calm, so he wouldn't punch me. "Look, man, I didn't mean to disrespect you. I think you know me better than that by now. The best way I can make you look good, as my sponsor, is to bust my ass for the other members whenever they need me to do something."

Just then, Baron came through the back door and paused a moment to give us his usual shit-eating grin. Hiney stared back at Baron before turning his eyes to me.

"When you're done with Baron's scoot," yelled Hiney, "you can start on mine."

With that, he stalked out of the kitchen, leaving a chuckling Baron alone with me. Keeping his gaze fixed on me the whole time, he pulled a bottle of vodka out of his inner vest pocket and took a good long swig before tucking it back in its standard place by his heart. Baron then walked over and slapped me on the shoulder.

"You just can't win, can ya, Prospect?"

"It's not about winning, Baron. It's about making your bike look good." I walked out back and through the rear garage door. As I made my way through the garage to where Baron's bike was parked in the driveway, the rumble of several bikes came growling around the bend. Baby Huey and Stroker pulled into the drive, and they didn't look happy. When we rode through town, we always had our war-face on, so we'd be left alone, but this was different—it was much deeper.

"What's up, Huey? Everything all right?" I asked.

"You're on a need-to-know basis, Prospect!" he snapped at me. "Who's in the house?"

"Hiney and Baron are inside," I answered. "Do you want me to go get them?"

"Just get ready to ride," Huey growled. Noticing the rags and cleaner in my arms, he added, "And get rid of that shit."

Huey marched purposefully to the front door with Stroker on his heels. I threw the rags down and walked over to my bike. Huey's foul mood had rubbed off on me. I knew I was only a prospect, but I hated being cut out of the loop like I was a nobody. I often had to bite my tongue to keep from saying what was on my mind and letting my pride ruin my chances.

The voices coming from inside the house grew very loud all of a sudden, and it sounded like a major argument was going down. Suddenly my desire to be a part of whatever was happening there faded. I pulled my bike away from the front curb and put the key in, so I would be ready to go.

With a bang, the front door was kicked open and all four members came running out. I started my bike and put her in first gear. Hiney jumped on his bike and pumped her to start her before looking over at me and yelling, "Where's your lid?"

In all the excitement, I had forgotten my helmet. I put my bike into neutral and leaned her over on her kickstand. I ran up to the garage and saw my skid lid on the work bench. I put it on as I ran back to my bike. Not ones to wait on a prospect, Hiney and the others were already down the road. I had some catching up to do. Lucky for me, my Sportster was a little hot rod compared to the Panheads they all were riding. I was on their asses in no time.

I shook my head in embarrassment—how could I have been so stupid as to forget my helmet when something was obviously going down? It was a mistake I couldn't afford to make. The stress must have been wearing on me. I had too much on my mind as it was, and now I was flying through town behind four hellbent bikers who seemed on a rampage for God only knew what reason.

After a few minutes of white-lining through traffic and dodging mirrors, it looked as though we were headed straight for the Backstreet Tavern—our main hangout—,but what the hell was the rush to get there?

Huey signaled for us to pull over into a vacant lot about two blocks from the bar. Huey got off his sled and made his way back to me.

"Don't get off that bike yet, Prospect. I have an important job for you."

"Sure, Huey," I said, swinging my leg back over the seat. "Anything."

"I want you to ride over to the Backstreet alone and check it out. I'm not riding blind into what could be a bad situation. We got word from the bartender that a group of Mad Dogs were in there. Find out who's there, how many, and where they're sitting in the bar. Can you handle that?"

"You got it."

"I need you back here fast and in one piece. You got that?"

"That's the plan, Huey," I said. "I'll be right back."

I had tried my best to sound confident, but my gut was in a knot the whole time. I rode off, not sure what lay ahead of me, but I needed to do this for the boys. As the bar came into view, I could see four bikes parked out front in the spaces reserved for the Noblemen's bikes—that took balls. But what worried me more was whoever that lone figure was that was standing out by the bikes. That was something prospects do. It had to be the Mad Dogs, but I still didn't know for sure.

I couldn't just pull in with the prospect standing lookout, so I rode past the bar for about a block and pulled in behind a mini-mall. With my bike parked between two cars, I ran down the alley and behind the buildings to find four more Harleys parked behind the laundromat. I took a cursory glance to make sure no bikers were simply doing a load.

My heart felt like it was beating through my chest. I was so pumped. This had to be a set-up, and we were one step ahead of it. I ran back to my bike, ready to ride back to where Huey and the others were waiting, but I wondered if this would be enough information for Huey. I started up my bike, still a bit unsure, but as I passed the bar, my gut told me that I had to find out more about what was going on *inside* our tavern.

Without much thought about what I was doing, I pulled into the Backstreet's parking lot and backed in next to the other bikes like I owned the place. The prospect took one look at my cut and immediately went to the front door and yelled inside. Over my engine, I couldn't tell exactly what he'd said, but it brought a few Mad Dogs out to see what was up.

"Well, what do we have here?" one of the Mad Dogs from inside said like some sort of cliché thug from a bad movie. "Are you lost?" His buddies plainly thought that his line was hilarious because they guffawed like idiots. "What are you doing here, asshole? Did your club send you here to make us leave?"

I wasn't paying much attention to their taunts. I was busy trying to figure out how to get past them and get inside. Then it came to me.

"Hell, I didn't know you guys were here. I'm here to relieve Matt," I said, mentioning the bartender. "He called me in early today. I guess you guys have him spooked."

Another Mad Dog narrowed his eyes and said, "You trying to tell me you work here? I call bullshit. What's your deal, punk?" He grabbed me by my vest, and it was all I could do to refrain from punching him square in the nose.

"Man, I've been working swing on-call for the last three months," I answered as innocently as I could muster. "Come on in, and I'll buy the next round of shots."

"I don't need you to buy shit," he said. "All I want from you is your cut."

He tried to pull my vest off, but I twisted away from him. He clocked me, and I went to the ground. I looked up at him and yelled, "Look, man, I need to get to work. If you want to kick my ass, at least do it inside while I'm on the clock."

If they don't believe this shit, my ass is dead.

Then one of the other Mad Dogs spoke up. "Snake, if the fool wants to buy us drinks, we might as well put down a few before we beat his ass."

Still looking skeptical, Snake said, "So, you're going to buy us a round of shots, huh? What would your club think about that?"

I shrugged, standing up and brushing myself off. "Hey, a man's got to make a living. And anyway, I'm hoping for a big tip."

I pushed my way through the Mad Dogs with all the nerve I could dig up and walked inside with the Mad Dogs right on my heels.

I hoped like hell that Matt would recognize me and pick up on my cues. If he didn't, this was going to end badly for me. I walked to the corner of the bar and saw that Matt was already nervous about what was going on. He looked at me, and I could tell that he was a little confused to see me walk behind the bar, but he didn't say anything.

"Hey Matt, I know I'm a little early," I said, patting him on the shoulder genially. "I was bored, and I knew you wanted to leave soon, so here I am. Don't worry about stocking the bar for me, I'll get it later. Just count out your drawer, and I'll take over now."

Matt looked at me then over at the Mad Dogs, who were waiting for his reaction. "Thanks, man," Matt said, finally. "It's all yours. Give me a second to count out."

"Where are those fucking drinks, Nobleman?" Snake roared. "And we want the top shelf stuff—none of that cheap shit!"

"I gotcha fellas," I said. "What's your poison?"

"Hey boys!" Snake yelled. "Come on out! Drinks are on the house!"

The restroom door opened with a bang, and four more Mad Dogs walked out. So, it *had* been a set-up. I knew it when I saw those other bikes out back.

"It's about damn time, Snake," one of the guys from the bathroom said as he took a place at the bar. "What the hell's going on?"

"We've got us a low-life Noblemen prospect, and he says the drinks are on him!" Snake grinned. "We'll drink his shit till his bros show up."

"Well all right then," said another member. "Set us up, asshole!"

As I reached for the glasses, I sized up the bunch of guys hugging my bar. I didn't even notice that I was shaking my head in disapproval.

"What's the matter?" one of the patches asked, narrowing his eyes. "You got a problem?"

"No problem fellas. It just seems like you all are looking for trouble. What are you doing here?" I asked, lining up the shot glasses.

"Just pour the drinks. You'll find out soon enough."

I ran the bottle of Jack Daniels across the line of glasses and poured myself a shot and tossed it back before putting the bottle back on its shelf.

As my patrons were toasting, I made my way into the back room where Matt was just finishing counting out his bank. I threw a glance over my shoulder to make sure no unwelcome ears were nearby.

"Hey Matt, thanks for covering for me. That could've gone bad. Listen, you need to get to the guys and tell them I've got eight Mad Dogs here, and they're about to pull up into an ambush. I'll try to keep them busy until you get back."

"Will do man. How far away are they?"

I told him that the guys were waiting just down the street. "Make sure Huey knows what's going on."

"Got it," he said. "Good luck, bud. I wouldn't want to be in your shoes right now."

"I don't really want to be in them either. Do y'all have any kind of weapons here? Maybe something behind the bar?"

Before Matt could answer, a Mad Dog burst in.

"What the hell is going on back here? We're thirsty!"

"Sorry, man. Just had to pick up my bank," I said.

I grabbed the cash register drawer from Matt and gave him a meaningful look before pushing past the patch and heading back out front. Matt left out the rear door with a Mad Dog on his ass. For a moment I was worried the Mad Dog would hop on his scoot and follow him home, but the patch sauntered back in just moments later. I was relieved until the reality of my situation set back in. I was alone in a bar with a shit-load of drunk, violent Mad Dogs who hated my guts. I just had to keep them distracted and stay alive long enough for my bros to get here and back me up.

"Throw some beers up on the bar, asshole, and hurry it up!" Snake shouted. As I opened some bottles that I knew were practically horse piss, he continued, "By the way, where's your club? We don't like being kept waiting."

"I don't know." I shrugged. "You expecting them or something?"

"Don't get cute. This is their bar, right?" Snake sneered. "I'm betting they'll be showing up anytime now."

"Some nights they do, and some nights they don't. You can never tell with those guys."

He barked a humorless laugh. "You better hope they show because it's your ass if they don't."

"It might be a while if they do." I said genially. "How about some juke box? It's on the house."

"No!" Snake shouted over the murmurs of the obviously bored Mad Dogs. "No fucking music. This ain't no pleasure trip!"

"Fine," I said. "What flavor beer do you want?"

"You know what, smart-ass?" He said, turning back to me. "Set up four pitchers. And we'll take another round of shots for everyone, too!"

As I poured, I looked around the bar, taking mental notes. I didn't like our odds—it was going to be two to one.

I sure hope Baby Huey knows what he's doing.

There were four guys at the pool table and four at the bar. I needed a plan. Matt seemed like he might have been about to say something before we were interrupted.

He's got to have something back here. I mean, shit, it's a biker bar!

I tried my best not to look like I was searching for something as I scanned the sticky shelves. Just then, I spotted a baseball bat with what looked like a five-inch crack running through the center of it. It was wrapped with duct tape to hold it together, but it was better than nothing if worse came to worse and I was on my own.

An eternity seemed to go by before I finally heard the comforting sound of a handful of Harleys pulling up. It was go-time. My mind was reeling as I tried to figure out how to handle everything.

I hadn't been the only one to hear my bros pull up. Snake yelled at the Mad Dogs around the pool table, "You four! Get in the restroom! I don't wanna spook them yet."

Tossing their pool cues aside, the four headed back towards the restroom just as the back door swung open. Baron strode in with his gun aimed at their heads.

"Everyone get your asses back to the bar," he commanded. When one of the Mad Dogs hesitated, he added, "Go ahead. Please give me an excuse. Now move!"

Baby Huey and Hiney walked through the front door with Stroker dragging a Mad Dog prospect in a chokehold behind them.

"All right," Huey yelled. "One stupid move from any of you motherfuckers, and it's going to get real ugly. Snake! Come on, man. We talked about this. I thought you were smarter! Why are you here?"

"Hey man," Snake said, holding up his hands, "tell your boys to relax. We just came for a couple of drinks."

"That's bullshit, and you know it," I yelled, staring Snake in the eyes. "You came in here to jump our asses."

"Prospect!" Huey snapped. "Shut the fuck up. I'll handle you later."

Snake stood up and walked over to Huey. "We haven't forgotten about what happened out at Bonnie Springs," Snake growled in Huey's face. "There will be payback." He looked over his shoulder at Baron's gun, then turned his gaze back to Baby Huey. "Just not today, it seems."

Baby Huey narrowed his eyes and chewed his lip before he came to a decision. “It’s your lucky day. I’m not in the mood for Mad Dog bullshit today. Now get your asses out of here before I change my mind.”

Stroker tightened his hold on the Mad Dog prospect, who groaned and tried to break away. Stroker held the hold until the prospects legs went limp; then he dropped him to the floor with a sickening thud.

“Come on, Huey!” yelled Stroker. “You’re not just going to let them walk out, are you?”

I thought Huey was going to shout at Stroker to shut up, but he just smiled a bit and turned to Snake, saying, “Do any of your boys want to get shot today?”

“Now we’re talking!” Baron whooped, cocking his S&W wheel gun.

Snake smiled, turned to the bar, and threw back the last shot of Jack. He tossed the glass to the floor where it shattered. “I’m bored. Let’s get the fuck out of this loser’s bar.”

Snake made as if to walk past Huey, but stopped and said in a low voice, “Next time, we’ll bring the artillery. You just raised the bar.”

“Obviously we can handle anything you throw at us,” Huey responded at a normal volume. “I don’t much care for gun play; I had enough of that in Nam, but I’ll be damned if I’m gonna walk into an ambush empty-handed.”

The Mad Dog prospect was starting to regain consciousness and was coughing where he still lay on the floor. Realizing the situation, he tried to stand up but wobbled a bit.

“Let me help you up,” Stroker said, putting the prospect back into a chokehold.

“Huey! Call off your boy. We’re leaving!”

Obviously choking back a laugh, Huey called out, “Stroker, let the probate go!”

Stroker released his hold but kicked the sputtering prospect in the ass, sending him stumbling into Snake.

"Get your low-life asses out of our bar," he said. "You're stinking the place up!"

Four Mad Dog patches made their way out the back door to their bikes with Baron at their heels, and Hiney and Stroker followed the others out the front door, which left Baby Huey staring at me.

"So, tell me something, Prospect," he said, crossing his arms. "What the hell were you thinking? Where were you going with this plan of yours?"

My mind went blank. "I don't know, Huey. I saw more bikes around back, and I just knew I had to get inside the bar and see what was going on."

I looked up at Huey and shrugged my shoulders. He was silent.

"Do you want a drink?" I asked.

"I sure do," he said, cracking a smile. "And get yourself one while you're at it. You did good, prospect. You did damn good."

Breathing a sigh of relief, I set up a draft for Huey and made myself a much-needed Jack and Coke.

"So what happened on your end?" I asked taking a seat beside him at the bar.

"Matt filled us in about the Mad Dogs hiding in the restroom, so we sent Baron around back to head them off. Stroker ran up on the prospect out front and took him out, so Hiney and I could ride our Harleys in with no problem. I'd say your plan worked."

"Well, to be honest, I didn't really have a plan," I said. "But I knew I had a good team backing me."

Baby Huey and I toasted and took a couple of long swigs from our glasses as the sound of the Mad Dogs' Harleys retreating slowly faded. We had our bar back. Baron came back in from the back alley as Hiney and Stroker walked in the front entrance.

"Hey Turk, Matt said to call him when it was safe to come back," Hiney said. "But for now, we have a new bartender!"

I set the beers up for everyone, and we all toasted. It was a proud moment for me with the club. I looked over at Baron. He just smiled that evil grin of his and tossed me a clean bar towel. I caught it just before it hit me in the face and looked down at it, confused.

"You did good, Prospect," Baron said with a laugh. "But you still need to clean my bike."

CHAPTER 3

BARON'S PUNCH

One cold December night, Dude, Shorty, and I were freezing our asses off outside the clubhouse while the members were holding their weekly meeting inside. We had to stand watch in case anything unusual came down the street or there was any movement in the desert behind the house.

We had been at our posts for several hours and decided to stand together for a moment to break the boredom. We joined up in a small circle and tried to stay warm while shooting the shit. The meeting was lasting longer than normal, and the cold was starting to get to me.

I was standing with my head down, looking at the ground when Dude said, "Shit."

He was staring past me with his eyes wide open. Suddenly, a sharp pain and a loud noise vibrated through my head. I lost my balance for a second and fell to one knee. Someone had just sucker punched me. I was expecting to get hit again, so I stood up as fast as I could and staggered a few steps away to get away from my assailant. I instinctively held up my hands and tried to focus on my opponent. Dude and Shorty were backing away. Why didn't they have my back?

My head was still throbbing and a twinge of pain was beginning to run down the back of my neck and shoulders when my vision finally focused on Baron fuming in front of me.

"What the fuck are you stupid motherfuckers doing?" Baron yelled. "What is this, some kind of party?"

A wave of anger ran through my veins, and my tightly clenched fists ached to punch Baron square in his fat nose. But I knew I had to control my anger—I was a prospect. "What the fuck, man?" I shouted, rubbing the knot that was rapidly forming on the side of my head.

Baron was still shouting, but it was just an annoying buzz in my ear at that moment. As my spontaneous rage subsided, I figured I had better pay attention to whatever he was barking at us.

"What if I had been a cop, or worse, what if I had been a Mad Dog? You would all be dead by now!" Baron yelled, shoving his finger in our faces.

"Baron," Dude said calmly, interrupting Baron's rant. "Man, we had a strong eye out tonight. We just now came together to warm up—"

"Shut your trap!" Baron spat. "When I want shit from you, I'll scrape it off your upper lip."

I was still rubbing the back of my head. I was definitely going to have a lump on my skull. "I think you've made your point, man. We've got it."

Baron whirled on me. "I'll let you know when I think you've got it, Prospect. If I ever catch you girls powdering your noses again, you'll be warming up in the hospital. Is that clear?"

We slowly started to back away from the asshole raging in our faces and head back to our posts, but Baron had other ideas.

"Wait a fucking minute! Did I say I was through with you scumbags?"

"What now?" I sighed under my breath as we turned back to Baron.

"I expected a little more from you, Turk," Baron growled. "Do you have a problem taking a punch when you get caught fucking up?"

"I always have a problem taking a punch for any reason, but you're the patch."

"I don't give a shit what you're good with, asshole," he yelled. "If punching you upside the head makes me feel good, I'm going to do it anytime I want. You got that, Prospect?"

"Well, if the pain in my head is any indication of how you feel, then you must feel pretty damn good," I said, trying to keep my tone even.

"Yeah, you're right," Baron said, rubbing his hands together. He allowed himself a small smile. "I love it when my knuckles bleed."

Baron's smile dropped as he turned an intimidating glare at the other two prospects.

"How about you guys? You want to help me feel better? My other hand feels left out. It needs to bleed also."

Dude was a big guy. He struck me as a no-bullshit, kick-your-ass-in-a-heartbeat kind of guy. He stepped into Baron's face, and I was expecting him to push back against Baron's degradation, but he just raised his arms out to the side and yelled jovially, "Hey, man, I'm game! Whatever it takes to make you feel better. Give it your best—"

Baron's fist cracked into Dude's temple in a left hook that sent him to his knees. Only a second passed before Baron sent his knee into Dude's forehead as he looked up. He was unconscious before he hit the ground.

Baron shook his fist in pain as he stood over Dude's motionless body. "Damn, that felt good. Thanks, Prospect, now I feel much better!" Shorty stared in disbelief as Baron turned to me and grinned. "You boys obviously need more discipline than you've been getting, and I'm willing to sacrifice my knuckles to help you out."

Baron turned on his heel and walked back across the yard to the clubhouse. I gave him the middle-finger salute for my own satisfaction. Still plainly shocked, Shorty knelt down beside Dude. Dude suddenly came to and shot up, swinging. Shorty jumped back, slapping at Dude's arms as they whizzed by his head.

"Woah, woah, woah! Calm down, Dude!" Shorty yelled. "It's over, man, he's gone!"

Realizing what had happened, Dude's face darkened. "That son of a bitch! I'm going to kill that motherfucker!" Dude shot past Shorty and me in a full-out sprint towards the back door of the clubhouse.

Oh shit.

If he made it inside, the guys would put him in the hospital, for sure, or maybe worse.

"Dude! Wait!" I shouted, running after him. I knew I wouldn't be able to catch up with him, but I had to try. Dude suddenly stopped and turned around, giving me the opportunity to tackle him to the ground.

"Get off me, Turk!" he yelled. "Do I have to kick your ass too?"

"Are you fucking crazy, man? You go in there acting like this, and you're a dead man!"

"Let me up, asshole. I'm done with this shit!"

"No, you're not. You're just so mad you can't think straight."

"What the fuck do you know, Turk? You think it's cool for him to just come out here and smack us around?"

"Who the fuck do you think you are, Dude?" I asked. "Baron or any other club member can come out here and do whatever the fuck they want. They went through this exact same shit when they prospected. No one cuts anybody any slack. You've got to remember that."

Dude had stopped struggling underneath me. He seemed to be calming down, and he got real quiet. I slowly stood up and held out my hand to him to help him up. He looked at it for a moment, considering, and then grabbed it tightly. I leaned back and pulled the massive man to his feet. Dude stared at the back door for a moment, then shook his head and slowly walked to the far corner of the yard to resume his post in silence.

"What d'ya think, Turk?" Shorty asked, coming up beside me. "Is Dude going to be okay with all this?"

"I don't know. Let's leave him alone for a while to sort his shit out," I said. "I think he'll be all right."

As midnight crept closer, the night air was getting colder and colder. *How much longer are those assholes planning on staying in there?* I thought.

Just then, the back door suddenly swung open. Hiney came out and made his way over to me. "Turk, I need to see you and the other prospects—now."

I turned to yell for Dude and Shorty, but they were already heading our way. I could tell Hiney wasn't happy.

"Baron said you guys were hanging out together and ignoring your posts," he said with a glare. "Is that right?"

Shaking my head, I said, "Nothing could be further from the truth. Baron was out of line for—"

"He's a punk-ass son of a bitch, and he'll get his!" Dude cut in.

"Hey! Watch your fucking mouth, Prospect! You're talking shit about a full patch, and that just doesn't happen!" Hiney yelled. "You hear me?"

Dude was so mad he couldn't even look Hiney in the eyes. He turned his head away and crossed his arms.

"Whatever you might think about a full-patch had better stay in that pea-brain of yours," Hiney said.

"Fuck this!"

Dude turned his back on Hiney and walked around to the front of the house. I figured he was going to throw his patch in, and that would be the end of that, but Hiney wasn't done with him yet—nobody disrespected a member of the club and just walked away.

"Turk," Hiney said, still glaring after Dude, "go get that fucking prospect and bring him back to me. I'll be in the house."

"You got it."

"I'm right behind you," Shorty called out.

As we rounded the corner to the front of the house, we saw that all the patches were congregated in the front yard. I searched the crowd for Dude and finally saw him by the street, talking to his sponsor, Big Dave.

Both men were intimidating to look at, each over six feet tall and hulking with muscle—neither of them were strangers to the weight bench. As for me, I rarely lifted; I was more of a heavy-bag kind of guy for the speed and power.

Dude was pleading his case to Big Dave, but he was plainly keeping an eye out for Baron. Just then, Baron came through the front door and pushed his way through the patches on the lawn to where his bike was. He never even noticed Dude, but Dude noticed him. His whole expression changed, and a cloud of fury passed over his face.

Baron leaned back against his scoot and pulled his vodka from its place in his inner vest pocket. As he unscrewed the cap, a couple of members walked up to him. They talked for a few minutes and had a short laugh. Baron took a couple large gulps from the bottle and tightened the cap before slipping it back inside his vest.

I was trying to make my way over to Dude as fast as I could, and as I approached, I heard him say, "I have to do this, Big Dave. I'm sorry, but I need to do this."

Big Dave grabbed for Dude's arm, but Dude twisted away from his grip and made a bee-line for Baron. Unable to stop him, Big Dave yelled over the noise of the crowd.

"Hey, Baron! Heads up, man!"

Baron didn't hear Big Dave's warning, but a bunch of other patches did, and they quickly jumped into action. They were going to make sure that whatever Dude had in mind wasn't going to happen.

Dude dodged the first attempt to grab him. He reminded me of a full-back with a football shoving his way through a crowd of players trying to tackle him. A second patch jumped on his back and tried to take him down, but Dude was too big. He was dragging several members with him as he trudged on towards Baron. It wasn't until Stroker ran into him like a line-backer that Dude was finally taken down. They all hit the ground and everyone else joined the dog pile.

Finally aware of what was happening, Baron pushed through the crowd and saw Dude lying under a pile of angry patches. He seemed to be unable to breath with all the weight on his chest, and Baron just smiled as Dude slowly began to lose consciousness.

Stroker, who was on top of Dude at the bottom of the pile, didn't like the weight pressing against him, either.

"Get the hell off me!" He wheezed. "What the fuck!"

As the members untangled themselves from the mound, Dude's face went from blue to bright red. When Stroker finally crawled off of his chest, Dude rolled over and coughed hard several times, gasping deeply.

"Fuck you! Fuck you all!" he screamed once he finally caught his breath.

"What's the problem, Prospect?" Baron asked in a mocking tone. "Can't handle club disciplinary actions?"

"Is that what you call what happened out back?" Big Dave said, stepping into Baron's face. "Disciplinary action?"

"You got that right," Baron said, all amusement gone from his face. "They abandoned their posts, so I set them straight. You have a problem with that, too?"

Big Dave and Baron pressed further into each others faces.

"If you ever have a problem with my prospect again, you come see me. I'll handle the punishment of the prospects I sponsor. You got that?" Big Dave shouted, sending spittle into Baron's face.

"Really?" Baron's eyes narrowed. "Is this some new rule you're making up? Because I've never heard of it."

Big Dave leaned forward and lowered his voice. "Let's just say that my new rule applies only to you."

Baron pulled away from Big Dave and clinched his fists in anger. I was waiting for him to swing at Big Dave, but just then Baby Huey pushed his way through the crowd.

"What the hell is going on over here?" he shouted as everyone quieted and turned to face him.

"Nothing really," Baron said, crossing his arms. "Except Big Dave is covering for his prospect's failure to stand his post." He pointed to the ground where Dude was still sitting. "I believe we need to reconsider allowing this man to wear a prospect's patch."

That got Dude to his feet. He turned to Huey. "For one, we did nothing wrong out back while standing post. And two," he looked at Baron, "I'm not just some punk that you can come out and pistol-whip anytime you feel like it. We were just standing our posts when you—"

"I think I've heard enough," Huey cut in. "We'll bring this matter up at the next meeting. It's already been a long night."

Baron stared at Huey in shock, "Shit, Huey, this won't take long! I'll tell you what's going on if you just—"

"I don't discuss club business out in public, and I need a drink right now, so shut the fuck up, Baron!" Huey looked over at Big Dave. "You've got a week to get your prospect straightened out. We'll vote on his prospect status next meeting. Keep your boy in line. Am I clear?"

"I've got it under control," Big Dave said sternly.

The severity fell instantly from Baby Huey's face as he threw his arm over Baron's shoulder and pulled him in with a grin. "Come on, bro, relax! Let's go have a drink."

"Beat you to it," Baron said as he held up his half-pint vodka. "Let's do one together."

Baby Huey grabbed the bottle from him with a smile and held it up, turning to look at the crowd of members.

"Here's to all my bros, now let's get the fuck out of here."

Everyone gathered around Huey and, one by one, took a swig before heading over to their bikes. The sudden roar of all the Pan and Shovelhead engines breaking through the still night air acted like a shot of adrenaline straight to my heart. It was going to be a long week for Dude, and I wouldn't want to be in his shoes. But I shook his situation from my thoughts and cranked my scoot. We were heading to the bar, and that's all I wanted to think about for the rest of the night.

CHAPTER 4

THE BLUE NOVA

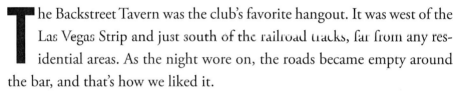

The Backstreet Tavern was the club's favorite hangout. It was west of the Las Vegas Strip and just south of the railroad tracks, far from any residential areas. As the night wore on, the roads became empty around the bar, and that's how we liked it.

Staring down the grim, empty street outside the pub sent a bleak peacefulness through my body. The darkness seemed to have a life all its own, and I felt like I owned it. I was the predator, and everyone else was prey. I was like a nocturnal beast, and I loved the mystery each night kept hidden in its shadows.

That's where I found myself most nights, watching over the members' bikes as they drank and partied inside. On occasion, I would send the other prospects inside the bar to stand guard over the patches, so I could have the night air to myself. It was one of the few times I could totally relax while on duty. Using the light from the star-filled sky and the cold gleam of the moon, I surveyed my nighttime kingdom, ready to pounce at any sign of irregularity.

As I sat outside alone late one winter evening, listening to the muffled shouts and laughing from my bros inside, I became aware of the growing sound of music approaching. I heard the music long before I saw the headlights of the vehicle responsible for interrupting my peaceful nightly reverie.

The dark blue Chevy Nova sped past the bar before suddenly slamming on its brakes. It came to a stop in the middle of the road where it idled for a moment. The reverse lights flickered on, and the transmission whined as the Chevy rapidly backed up This was definitely out of the ordinary, and anything unusual around here is generally not a good sign. I was ready to head for the door and yell in at the guys, but I hesitated.

The blue Nova stopped in front of the bar. I waited for something to happen, but it just sat there with the music pounding at the windows as if it were desperately trying to get out. The transmission clunked back into drive, and the car started to pull into the driveway.

This didn't sit right with me, so I got off my bike and walked over to the front door in case I needed to alert my bros. I hesitated again, though. I didn't want to look stupid if this turned out to be just another customer.

What the hell are you up to? I thought.

The Nova parked beside our bikes. Now that they were closer, the inside of the car was more visible, and I was relieved to see two blondes laughing and dancing to their music—at least, they were until they saw me approaching the driver's side window. The two women fell silent, and the driver slowly reached over to turn off the radio.

Upon realizing that I'd have to make the first move, I tapped on the window, flashed my best smile, and gestured for them to roll the window down. The driver looked over at her friend, shrugged, and looked back at me with a frightened smile.

"You girls look like you're having a good time," I said as the window slid slowly down. "What's the occasion? Just Saturday night?"

Neither of them answered but turned to look at each other as if they couldn't believe I was talking to them. The driver looked past me at our bikes before turning her big blue eyes back to me.

"I didn't park too close to the motorcycles, did I?" she asked sweetly.

"Nope, you're good!" I said, leaning in to get a better look at them.

The driver had long blonde hair and large hoop earrings. My eyes traveled the length of her, from her neck down to where her low-cut black dress had ridden up to the tops of her thighs. She felt my gaze and immediately tugged her dress down to try and cover her overly exposed legs, but the dress wasn't having it, and it sprung right back into place. Our eyes met again, and when I gave her another smile, this time she returned it.

"What brings you to this side of town, ladies?"

"Well, I don't know if I should tell you this, but—"

"We're here on a dare," the passenger cut in, leaning over to look at me.

"Anna!" the driver yelled. "That's not cool!"

Anna's black dress was longer than her friend's, but it had a slit all the way up the side, exposing the fish-net stockings she wore on her long, shapely legs.

"So, what was the dare?" I asked, turning back to the driver.

"Well, I saw a couple of you guys riding your choppers down the street last night, and I thought it would be cool to maybe take a ride, sometime."

"That does sound like fun. Did someone dare you to do it tonight?" I asked.

"Exactly," the driver said. "I told our friends at the club tonight what I wanted to do, and they laughed and dared me to do it. They said I didn't have the nerve."

I smiled devilishly. "I might be able to help you prove them wrong."

The driver grabbed her friend's hand and squeezed it, saying nervously, "Maybe we should just leave."

"What, and go back to your friends with your tail stuck between your legs? Come on. You're here," I said genially, "so you might as well come in and at least have a drink."

They looked like they were considering it until I heard voices behind me. Dude and Shorty had evidently decided to come check up on me.

Shit. Bad timing, I thought as they spotted me by the car.

"Hey Turk!" Dude called out. "Whatcha hiding over there?" He started towards me, trying to see around where I stood. A wicked, knowing grin spread across his face when he saw the two girls.

"Who-o-o-oa!" Dude said, stretching the word like a catcall. "What have we here, Turk?" Dude shoved past me and leaned down with his face through the window.

I stepped back to give Dude a chance with the girls. Then I noticed that Shorty had made his way over to the passenger's window and was starting in on the other girl. The two of them looked like a pair sharks during a feeding frenzy.

"Come on in girls," Dude purred, opening the door a crack. "We'll show you a good time."

"I don't think so," the driver said, pulling her door shut. "I think it's time we left."

"Come on!" Dude said, obviously a little perturbed. "You can't leave. You just got here!" He pulled the door open again.

"Please just leave us alone," the driver said frantically. "Let go of the door!"

The tone of her voice made it clear that she was scared. I had seen and heard enough. These guys were just terrorizing the poor girls. I stepped up to Dude and put my hand on his shoulder. "Hey, Dude," I said. "Back the fuck off, man. Leave them alone."

Dude released the door handle, straightened up, and turned his hulking frame to face me. He shoved a meaty finger into my chest, yelling, "Fuck you, Turk! You can't keep them all to yourself. I'll do what I want, and right now I want to—Argh!"

I had shoved my elbow dead center into his chest—I was tired of him poking me. Dude stumbled back a few steps, rubbing his ribs. I saw Shorty staring at me over the roof of the car in disbelief.

"What the hell is wrong with you, Turk?" yelled Shorty.

"These girls are with me, and you guys are way out of line," I answered. I looked back at Dude and knew instantly that I'd fucked up.

"So, you're gonna try and take me out over some woman, asshole?" he growled.

"No, man," I said, holding up my hands to try and placate him. "It's nothing like that. It's just that you were scaring them, and when you got up in my face, I over-reacted, that's all."

"That's bullshit, man!" Dude yelled. "I've had it with your crap! I should kick your ass right now…but I have a better idea." He signaled for Shorty to follow him. Shorty came around the car, watching me carefully the whole time. They disappeared inside the bar. As soon as the double doors swung shut, the girls started thanking me.

"Oh my God!" the driver cried out. "I totally thought they were going to try and attack us!"

"What makes you think you're safe with me?" I asked, trying to be scary. "Maybe I was just saving you for myself."

"Oh," she said, her thankful air suddenly replaced by annoyance. "So you're going to turn into an asshole now too?"

"No. I just think that if you two were to come in now, it would be trouble," I said, rubbing the back of my head. "You know what I mean?"

"So you want us to leave." It wasn't a question. "Wow—a bad boy with a big heart. Well, if you say so. We'll be leaving now."

"Wait! I didn't get your name. How will I find you to give you that ride?"

She smiled. Boy, I was glad to see it again. "I'm Jody, and this is Anna. I guess we'll head back over to the Trapdoor. If you're not busy later, why don't you stop by?"

"So, you have no trouble being seen with a biker in that joint with all your friends around?" I asked.

Anna leaned over Jody's lap. "I think it would be so cool for you to come see us there. Our friends would totally freak out! Come see us, please!" she begged.

"The Trapdoor, huh?" I said. "We'll see if I can get away later. I don't know what's waiting for me on the other side of those doors. You two might've gotten me into a lot of trouble." I winked.

"Oh, I hope not!" Jody said. "Please try and make it. It will be fun—I promise!"

"Oh yeah?" I said, leaning closer through the window. "Prove it."

She slid her hands through my hair and pulled me slowly to her lips. Her mouth opened as our lips met, and I tasted her for the first time. Her fingers tightened in my hair as I slid my hand through the window and down across the curves of her dress.

"Damn, Jody!" Anna whooped. "You're out of control!"

Jody couldn't help but laugh in the middle of our kiss. I smiled. With one more short kiss, I pulled my head out of the window and regained my composure.

"Hmm, maybe I *will* come find you tonight."

Jody smiled, started the car, and said. "If you don't make it, I guess it'll just be your loss." She backed out and headed out to the street. Within seconds, the music was blaring as they sped down the dark road without looking back. I smiled and shook my head.

What the hell just happened?

I looked back at the door to the bar and wondered what was waiting for me. Thankfully, I couldn't go in at the moment because someone had to be outside with the bikes. But I knew they'd let me know soon enough how badly I'd fucked up. The shit could hit the fan real quick with the club, and since I had a very low tolerance for bullshit, it happened often with me.

I knew Dude was inside making a big deal out of what had gone down. Since he was in the shit with the club because he had disrespected Baron a couple nights ago, this was his chance to take some of the heat off himself and make me look bad instead.

I had been standing outside for what seemed like forever when the door finally swung open. It was Stroker, and he didn't look happy.

"Do you know who I am and what I do," he yelled. Stroker was the Sergeant at Arms, which meant he was the disciplinarian.

"Yes," I said, nervously. "You're the one who straightens shit out when things go wrong. Look, I don't know what Dude told you, but—"

"Shut the fuck up, Prospect," Stroker shouted, sending spit flying. "I don't give a damn what you have to say. You just stand there and be quiet! You got that?"

I nodded, but I was boiling inside. It wasn't in my nature to let someone tell me to shut up. But I stood eye to eye with him and bit my tongue. I could tell that he was sizing me up as we stood face to face. Stroker was one of the first members I had met when Hiney brought me to the clubhouse for the first time. I had helped him install a Weber Carburetor on a XLH Sportster, and I thought that should count for something, but as a prospect, you're never an equal.

"I understand that you hit another prospect over a woman. Is that correct?" he fumed.

"I can understand how Dude might see it that way, but no, that's not what happened."

"Oh, really?" Stroker said, raising his brows. "So, you're going to set me straight, I take it."

I had to be really careful with my words here. The wrong tone or any inkling of disrespect could put me in the hospital.

"I wanted to impress you and Baby Huey by bringing a couple of chicks to your table, but Dude was scaring them off."

To my surprise, Stroker laughed. "That's good, Prospect. That's real good." He turned and looked, for a moment, as if he were headed back inside, but then he said, "But not good enough." He spun around and punched me square in the jaw.

I could have dodged the hit, but if I had blocked it, the consequences would have been far worse, so I let it happen. The punch knocked me on my ass, and I decided it best to just lie there for a moment and act hurt.

Stroker leaned over me and yelled, "Now get your punk ass up. You're not fucking hurt, and I'm far from done with you!"

I rolled to the side and pushed myself up. I guess his punch had done a little more damage than I had anticipated. A wave of pain rode up the back of my neck and into my head. I hesitated for a moment to clear my head, but I had to snap out of it quickly. I finally got to my feet and stood eye-to-eye with Stroker again.

"All right," I said, my ears still ringing. "I was wrong. Now what?"

"'Now what?'" Stroker mimicked as he jabbed me in the chest with a stiff finger. "I've got your 'now what.' Wait here!"

Stroker walked back to the doors, shoved them open, and yelled, "Dude! Get your prospect ass out here!"

Dude came out and walked over with Stroker to where I was standing. Stroker slapped him on the back of the head and pointed at me. "Here's your chance, man," said Stroker. "Go take his vest from him."

Dude's eyes went wide and the color dropped from his face. No man who wanted to stay alive would willingly give up his vest. Dude knew I would fight him like my life depended on it. I never dreamed it would go this far, but it was up to Dude to make the first move.

"Hey, man, shit!" Dude choked out. "I was just pissed he made me look bad in front of those girls. I didn't mean for it to cost him his patch."

That was the wrong thing to say. Stroker grabbed Dude by the throat and slammed him against the wall.

"You're on thin ice, Prospect!" Stroker yelled into Dude's face. "You drag me out here to clean up your mess and then say never mind?" Still grasping him by the throat, Stroker tossed Dude at me. I extended my arms out catch him, so he wouldn't knock us both back into our bikes. After we regained our balance, we waited for Stroker's next move.

"I don't have time for this shit," Stroker said. "You two fight it out during the next meeting, and the loser will be dragged out into the street without a vest. I'd take your vests now, but I think I'll make your lives a living hell before next Wednesday. Stay the fuck out here. I don't want to see the two of you for the rest of the night."

I gave Dude a long hard stare, and he knew he had it coming. He turned away from me and shook his head. After slowly walking over to his bike and sitting down sidesaddle on it, he said, "Sorry Turk. I had no idea Stroker would take it this far."

"Are you fucking kidding me, Dude?" I yelled. "Just what the hell did you expect? Now, I'm going to have to kick your ass next week."

"Oh, is that a fact?" Dude said, rising to his feet. "Why don't we just get it over with now? We'll see who kicks whose ass."

"You're such a fucking dumb-ass. You just can't wait to piss Stroker off again, can you? You better go home and practice falling down because that's what you're going to be doing a lot of when we fight."

Shorty, who had just come through the doors, laughed and said, "That's good, Turk! 'Practice falling down.' I like that!"

"Shut up, Shorty," Dude barked. "Real funny, Turk. I'm so scared."

He pushed up from his bike and walked over to the other end of the bikes to get further away from me. He leaned back against the wall with his arms folded and looked off in the other direction. Shorty looked at Dude then back over to me.

"What are you waiting for?" I said gruffly. "Get down there with your buddy."

"Yeah? Well, fuck you too, Turk," Shorty grumbled as he walked over to Dude. As soon as he leaned on the wall next to him, Dude shoved him away.

"Go bother someone else and leave me the fuck alone," he shouted.

Shorty gave Dude the middle finger salute and walked over to his bike.

I sat down on my bike and pulled out my blade. I sat there playing with my knife for almost an hour when the bar door finally swung open and the music from the bar poured into the parking lot.

Baby Huey came out first, followed by Stroker, Big Dave, Rotten Ralph, and Hiney. I stood up out of respect and waited for my orders. Stroker slapped Huey on the shoulder and pointed at me.

"See, we would've had a quiet night if it hadn't been for that prospect over there. He started a bunch of shit with the other prospects earlier. What do you think we should do Huey?"

With a breath of a laugh, Huey said, "Sounds to me like he's a lot like you." He casually pushed Stroker's arm off his shoulder.

"What's that supposed to mean?" Stroker was obviously trying not to look too offended.

"Well, prospects need to vent too, Stroker."

"Yeah, well, not while I'm out drinking," Stroker said. "They can do it on their own time."

Huey smiled. "Is this one of your new rules? Just leave the prospects alone. I had a good time tonight, and now you want to screw that up. It's over. Let's go home."

The look Stroker gave Huey would have preceded his fist slamming into their nose, but it was aimed at Huey, so he just slowly exhaled and walked over to his bike.

The club didn't like officers to ride alone without another patch or prospect riding with them. The members were getting ready to leave, so I walked over to Baby Huey to see what he wanted me to do. He saw me walk up and pointed to Stroker.

With a wicked grin, he said, "Follow Stroker home, then take the rest of the night off."

That was music to my ears. Stroker was pulling out on his Sportster before I even had my bike started. I got my scoot running and fish-tailed out of the parking lot. Stroker never acknowledged my presence as he throttled hard down the dark streets. He was driving like a maniac, no doubt trying to lose me, and it took all my skills to keep up with him. I had never ridden this hard before, and Stroker was giving me a quick lesson in high-speed cornering. My heart was pumping pure adrenaline at twice the speed of my bike. I was down shifting into the corners and power shifting out of them. I was putting my XLH Harley through the paces, and even with the eight-over front end, she handled the turns very well.

As Stroker pulled into his neighborhood, a wave of pride surged through me—I had managed to keep up.

Stroker pulled onto his driveway and shut his motor down. As he stepped away from his bike, he motioned for me to come over. He still looked pissed, so I mentally prepared myself for another ass-chewing.

"I've got my eye on you, Prospect. I think you have potential, but I'm cutting you no slack. You hear me, man? You fucked up tonight!"

"I got it, Stroker. I can fix this."

"Good! I expect you to kick Dude's ass next week. You got that?"

"Yeah, that fucker's going to pay for talking shit about me."

"There's a lesson to be learned here besides who wins the fight. I hope you can figure that out before next week."

I paused a moment to think about it. That was the last thing I had expected to hear from him. Was Stroker trying to discipline us or educate us?

"Now get the fuck out of here," he said, jerking his head in dismissal.

I walked back to my Harley, which was still cracking from the heat of the exhaust cooling off. I looked back at Stroker a final time. He gave me a swift nod goodbye and turned to go inside.

That nod meant the world to me. I felt myself breathe for the first time that night. As I pulled out of the neighborhood, the cool desert night air hit me and I felt great. All I could think about was getting to the Trapdoor and feeling Jody's lips on mine again.

CHAPTER 5

DAMNED DAM

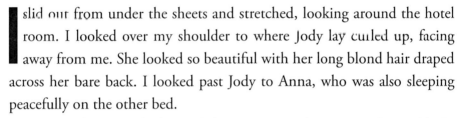

I slid out from under the sheets and stretched, looking around the hotel room. I looked over my shoulder to where Jody lay curled up, facing away from me. She looked so beautiful with her long blond hair draped across her bare back. I looked past Jody to Anna, who was also sleeping peacefully on the other bed.

Last night, Anna had stayed down stairs in the casino, playing blackjack while Jody and I came up to the room and got to know each other better. We must have been passed out when she came up. I never heard her come in.

Most of the night was a blur, but I remember riding to the hotel with Jody holding tightly onto me from the back of my Harley. After talking to her for a while at the Trapdoor, I found out that they were from California and were spending the weekend here with some friends from work.

I rubbed my head and headed towards the bathroom, passing Anna's bed. She was lying half-covered in the sheets with her long, tanned legs hanging out. Just enough of her white panties were visible to send my imagination running wild.

I smiled and shook my head. *Just keep walking, Turk*, I thought.

After the bathroom, I sat on the edge of Jody's bed and tried to gently wake her by rubbing her back. She moaned, grabbed my arm, and pulled it around her waist as she rolled over. I kissed her a few times on the side of the neck and shoulder and forced myself to get back up. I wanted to stay, but I had business to take care of.

I decided to just leave my number and hit the road. As a prospect, I was always on call, and I needed to check in. It may have been Sunday, but it was a seven-days-a-week kind of deal, and you couldn't just disappear on the weekend.

With a jolt I remembered where I had parked my bike. I walked over to the window and looked down onto Third Street from the eighth floor. *Whew, there she is,* I thought. I would have thought they would have towed her by now, but I must have been luckier than I thought. The night before I was full of Jack, and nothing else mattered but getting up to the room with Jody.

I paused in the doorway and took another glance back at Jody before slowly shutting the door behind me.

Thirty minutes later, I was walking into my house to the phone ringing. I figured it was Hiney wanting to know where the hell I was. I plopped down on the couch and answered the phone, mentally preparing myself for a good scolding.

"Why did you leave so early, baby?" Jody's sweet voice surprised me. "You didn't even say goodbye."

"I'm sorry, Hon," I answered gently. "I wanted nothing more than to have stayed longer and cuddled with you, but I'm already in a ton of trouble with the club, and I had to check in."

"Oh well. I understand. We have to leave for home soon, anyway. You think you'll make it out to California some day?"

"Sure, baby, I go to Cali all the time. I'll look you up, and we'll do dinner."

"That'd be nice." I could hear the smile in her voice. "I have to go now—my friends are telling us to hurry up, and Anna wants to gamble some more before we leave. I hope I'll see you soon. Let me give you my number."

I wrote down her address and number before hanging up. I was already mentally planning a trip down to L.A. to visit her.

Leaning back into the couch to get as comfortable as possible, I called Hiney. His voice brought me back to reality. In three days, there'd be a club meeting, and Dude and I were on the chopping block. It seemed to Hiney that I wasn't as concerned about it as he was—that just pissed him off even more.

"You better get your head on straight before Wednesday night, Turk!" Hiney yelled.

"You're right, man," I said. "I promise I won't embarrass you. Do you need to see me today?"

"Of course I do! Get your ass over here."

"I'm on my way. Be there in a minute." I hung up and threw my jacket back on.

I had known what I was getting myself into when I put on this prospect patch. I wanted to make full patch so bad I could taste it. There was nothing anyone could do to make me change my mind about joining the Noblemen. I knew it might take a year or longer to become a full member, but there was no way I was giving up.

Hiney was standing beside his scoot in the street when I pulled up. The minute he saw me, he put on his skid lid—apparently, he already had plans for the day. I pulled up beside his bike and stopped, idling.

"We have people from Arizona coming into town," Hiney yelled over my loud pipes. "We need to meet them at Hoover Dam."

Any time we had bros riding in from out-of-state, we would meet them at the state line to escort them in. It was just the kind of respect we had for each other. Prospects usually did this alone, so it was nice to have Hiney keep me company.

I rode alongside Hiney's 1951 Harley Panhead rigid-framed beast on my 1972 Harley Sportster XLH. I had been riding consistently for almost four years but on Harleys for less than two. My first Harley, a 1971 Sportster XLCH, had been stolen about nine months after I had bought her. That was how I met Hiney.

I was much happier with my new Harley, but my gut tightened every time I thought about that son of a bitch who stole my first Sportster. I figured the bike was in pieces by now, but I still needed to find the asshole who had taken her. The only way I would find peace would be to find the punk and make him pay. I wanted blood for my bike—lots of it. There would be retribution.

I had initially started hanging around the club to see if one of them had been the thief, but I soon found out that this bunch of guys wasn't into stealing Harleys. I could have moved on from there, but I stuck around. In the short time I had started riding with the Noblemen, I had seen the brotherhood and respect they shared between members, and that appealed to me. Hiney might not have led me to my chance at vengeance, but he did lead me to my brothers.

We tore through town, heading east toward Boulder City. Sportsters were smaller than the big twin Harleys, but they boasted speed and power the others couldn't match. Even the new Shovelhead Harleys had trouble keeping up with me.

We were about an hour ahead of schedule, and a beer sounded good. Boulder City had one bar, so that was where we headed. As we backed our bikes up to the curb, I felt a wave of warm air hit my back as it flowed out into the street from the open bar door. We made our way straight to the bar. Halfway through our first beers, Hiney told me the plan.

"You and Dude are in a lot of shit right now," Hiney started. "And as your sponsor, I'm responsible for your actions. If things go bad Wednesday night, I could get my ass kicked too, not to mention being thrown out if it's bad enough."

Hiney had every reason to be mad at me. I knew I couldn't guarantee the outcome of the fight, so I just nodded solemnly.

To wear the clubs bottom rocker was a huge responsibility, and I accepted that responsibility for the chance to prove that one day I was worthy of wearing the full set of colors of the club I loved. You must be willing to demonstrate to everyone that you have the will and the heart to fulfill your duties to the club as a prospect. A large part of being a prospect is being ready to serve the members at anytime and anywhere.

If a club member came at you like he was going to fight you or if he uses physical force to punish you, you must always show respect but also stand your ground. You can never show any disrespect, whine, or cower. The brotherhood was looking for good, strong, smart men in their ranks, not someone who would embarrass the club. You are being watched by everyone to see how you handle problems with other bikers or clubs. In this life with the club, you live in the extremes. It's about being a part of something much bigger than yourself.

"So, tell me, Turk," Hiney said. "What do you think is gonna go down on Wednesday night?"

"Well," I said, "I guess I'm going to have to fight Dude. He's the one who has a problem with me."

Hiney tipped his beer to his lips and took a nice, long swallow. After wiping his mouth with the back of his hand, he leaned forward and shoved his finger into my chest.

"Win or lose, that's just the beginning of your problems. I guess it's my fault. I haven't been tough enough on you." Hiney's brows furrowed deeper. "Here's what's going to happen. You're on your own from here on out. I'll wait here while you go and meet our brothers at the dam."

"How long till they get here?" I asked.

"Doesn't matter. You wait for them," Hiney answered firmly. "You hear me? You wait for them and then bring them here."

"Okay, I got it. Look, Hiney, no matter what it takes, I'm going to fix this shit."

"You'd better," he said. "This may be the last time you fly that prospect patch. You're being closely watched from here on out. That's all I have to say."

I didn't feel the need to say anymore, so I finished my beer in a quick chug and walked outside. I sat on my bike a few minutes in case Hiney ran out with some last-minute details for me, but when he didn't come out, I started my bike and sped off.

I was mad and confused as I tore down the road, but I knew it was more about my pride than actually being angry with Hiney. Most of all, I was disappointed in myself because I had let Hiney down and put him on the spot. I cruised through Boulder City and out past Lake Mead, considering my situation the whole way.

It was noon when I arrived. I rode across the dam into Arizona and up the steep narrow road to the refreshment stand that overlooked Lake Mead and the intake towers. I was sure glad it wasn't summer; the heat, as I sat exposed in the desert sun, would have been unbearable. It was a cool winter day, and I was more than comfortable in my leather jacket. I sat down and put my back to the short block wall that separated the parking lot from the cliff. I looked at my watch. *They should be arriving anytime now,* I thought. I had figured that this would be an easy job for the club, but I didn't realize how wrong I was.

I had made over a half a dozen trips to the store and restroom by the time the desert sun had begun to set. I was starting to get a little stressed out.

Did I miss them? Did they cancel their trip? Did they break down on the road? Should I go looking for them? And where the hell is Hiney? Is he still waiting at the bar? Has he heard from them? Surely, he'd find a way to tell me if he found out plans had changed. I was driving myself crazy. I had a decision to make and whatever that was, it had better be for the good of the club.

During my numerous trips back and forth into the store, I had noticed a pay phone on the wall. I thought about calling Hiney but realized that I didn't know the number to the bar where he'd been waiting. I also briefly considered calling the clubhouse, but I shook off the thought quickly; all they would do is chew my ass out for being impatient. I just had to wait until they showed up.

As 9 o'clock rolled around, I was a nervous wreck. The sun had long since set, and the frosty air was penetrating my leather jacket. The store had closed a few minutes earlier, but I needed to get warm, so I started my bike. After a few minutes, I was enjoying the comforting warmth from the jugs of my V-Twin engine. Once I could feel my hands again, I slipped them back inside my gloves and shut the motor down. I sat snuggled next to my Harley in the silence of the desert, enjoying the peaceful night air. I might have been on thin ice with the club, but at that moment, I found comfort in the fact that I knew I was right where they wanted me to be.

I tried to relax, but my mind was still racing. I couldn't stop thinking about them broken down somewhere on the way. I needed to go look for them. I started my bike and pulled to the edge of the parking lot. It was just a dark, two-lane road all the way to Kingman, so I wasn't worried about missing them. A semi-truck rolled past me and gave me a blast from his airhorns. I made the left turn out onto the highway and throttled through the gears, pressing ever deeper into Arizona. I hit my high-beam as I shot past the big rig, and the road opened up to me.

About 35 minutes later, just before 10, I pulled into the little café called Rosie's. I parked in front of the wooden porch. A waitress was just about to lock up when she saw me. She stuck her head out the door and yelled, "If you want something to eat, you're out of luck. I'm sorry but we're closing."

"What about a beer?"

She smiled sweetly and waved for me to come in. Not too many people treated bikers so kindly, but Rosie's Café was different. They catered to truckers and bikers and understood our ways. She gave me two beers, and I handed her a five and told her to keep the change. I walked back out onto the porch with my beers, so I could keep a good eye on the road. I knew that, with my luck, if I stayed inside to keep warm, they would go flying by.

The waitress followed me outside and took the beer I handed her. The porch light lit up her smiling face as she sat down next to me.

"It must be so cool to live in Vegas," she said with an eager giggle when I told her. "What are you doing way out here?"

"Just taking a break from the big city," I answered. "I need to do that every now and then."

"Do you work in one of the big casinos?"

"Not really, it's a smaller one downtown," I said. "I work at the Mint Hotel."

"I bet you see a lot of famous people, huh?"

"Eh," I said, shrugging. "Vegas isn't necessarily as glamorous as they make it seem in the movies. Folks there are just trying to make a living like everyone else."

She seemed a little disappointed by my answer, but she smiled anyway.

"I've been to Vegas a few times, but I wasn't 21 yet, so there wasn't much I could do," she said. "And I haven't been back since."

"Well, unless you play the slot machines or table games, it'll still be boring."

"Sounds like you're trying to talk me out of going to Vegas," she said with just a hint of a pout.

"Sweetheart," I said. "Why do you think I'm way out here tonight?"

"I don't know, "she said as she leaned over and whispered. "Are you going to tell me?"

"No," I whispered back. I tried to look playfully dangerous as I said, "If I told you, I'd have to kill you."

She laughed and slapped me on my shoulder. "I have to get back inside and help clean up. It was nice talking to you."

"You too. Maybe I'll stop by again soon."

"Sure, but make it a little earlier next time."

She pulled the door shut, and I heard the latch lock. It wasn't long after she'd left that the cold crept back in. I considered my situation as I sat alone in the dark. I knew I couldn't go much further on my tank of gas. My Sportster tanks held just about two and a half gallons of gas, which would get me about 100 miles on a good day. It was almost 11 o'clock, and I decided to make the cold ride back to the dam.

As I pulled back into the parking lot a half hour later, part of me hoped to see the other guys standing there looking for me, but of course, that wasn't the case. I wasn't sure what to do, so I sat down in the same spot I was before and got comfortable. I didn't know how long it would be before they arrived or even if they were going to, but I needed to get some sleep either way; I had to work tomorrow. Work was the least of my problems, though. If I had somehow screwed up and missed bringing these guys into town, the club would be done with me for sure.

I was just drifting off around midnight when the rumble of a Harley came echoing through the mountains. And what a beautiful sound that was. I stood up and tried to hear which direction the Harley was coming from, but the echo made it difficult.

When the headlights rounded the curve of the mountain on the Nevada side, my hopes fell. Even as it got closer across the dam, I couldn't make out what type of Harley it was. The bike disappeared behind the last cliff as it pulled hard up the steep road to where I was. When the bike topped the crest, I could finally tell who it was—Hiney. Part of me was relieved to see him, but another part told me that I had permanently fucked up.

Hiney shut his motor down next to mine. He stepped away from his bike and with a huge grin, opened his arms to me. Thank God I wasn't in trouble. We embraced and slapped each other hard on the back a few times. Hiney grabbed my shoulders and looked at me at arm's length.

"I'm so proud of you, Turk!" Hiney said, sounding like a proud father. "I'm so glad you're still here."

"Of course, I'm still here," I said, only a little confused. "You sent me here to meet some bros, right?"

"There's no one coming!" Hiney grinned mischievously. "This was a test—a test to see if you would stay here till they showed up, no matter how long it took, without question. You didn't give up on me,;you stayed. You did good man; you did good!"

"You mean I sat out here for 12 hours for nothing?"

"No, asshole," he yelled, a bit of annoyance coloring his voice. "You get to keep your patch tonight because you did what you were told without question. Is that patch nothing to you?"

"No, my patch is my life. It means everything to me. Sorry, Hiney. I'm cold and worn out. I'll do whatever it takes to keep my patch."

His frown relaxed, and he smiled again. "What you did tonight was the first step toward keeping your patch. But you really need to stay on top of your game from now on. Is that clear?"

"Yes," I said. "Very clear, but can we please go home now?"

"Yeah," he laughed slapping me on the back again. "Let's get the hell out of here!"

The ride home was freezing, but my heart was warm, knowing I had done what the club expected of me. Riding next to Hiney always made me proud of what I wanted to accomplish—to full patch with the club, no matter what it took.

CHAPTER 6

DUDE'S DEAL

I was glad and worried at the same time. My stomach was in knots, but I was glad it was finally Wednesday night and the waiting was over. I really didn't know what was expected from Dude and me tonight. From what I had gathered from all the threats and yelling, we were to fight for our patches tonight. If that was the case, I was going to have to hurt him, and I didn't much like that idea. I had see prospects come and go over the last few months, but Dude, Shorty, and I were hanging tough through it all. I needed to put on blinders. I needed to quit worrying about everyone else and focus on my objective to become a full patch.

Members were starting to trickle in one by one for the weekly meeting. Hiney pulled up on his Panhead, and I walked over to greet him. He backed his rigid-framed Harley to the curb and stepped over the seat. Pulling off his skid lid, he held his hand out for me to stop.

"Not now, Turk," Hiney said gruffly. "We'll talk later."

Suddenly, I felt alienated from the club. I stepped back into the yard and felt like everyone's eyes were on me. It was one of those moments you just felt like you didn't belong. Everyone was in the yard talking before the meeting like normal, but somehow, it felt different this time.

Dude and Shorty weren't there yet, so I seemed to be the subject of the conversations in the yard. Every time I approached a group of members, they shook their heads and turned their backs to me. Any attempt to engage in a conversation was ignored. I was beginning to think that no matter what the outcome of the fight turned out to be, this would be my last night to wear the bottom rocker.

No use being a pussy about this, I thought. *Put your war face on and take it as it comes.*

From my solitary vantage point, I watched as two more bikes backed in. It was Big Dave and Dude. I turned and scanned the yard for Hiney, but he was nowhere to be found.

At least Dude has his sponsor's support, I thought. *Looks like I'm on my own.*

The cold breeze cut though my open leather jacket, so I found the zipper and yanked it up before reaching into my pockets and pulling out my gloves. As I was putting on the second glove, a hand slapped me firmly on the back.

"Tonight could make or break you, Turk," Stroker said following my gaze to where Dude stood talking intensely to Big Dave. "We're going to see if you have what it takes. You ready?"

"I'm out to make this club my life," I answered. "I'm always ready."

One side of his lips turned up in a begrudging half-smile. "We'll see man. I just don't know if you've got what it takes to full patch. You need to turn this shit around. But I guess we'll see."

I really could have used some bolstering, but all I was getting was a big cold shoulder. The members made it seem like no matter what I did, it wasn't enough. It was a constant beat down, but I was determined to win.

I've come this far, and I'm not quitting. If they want me out, they're going to have to kick my ass and drag me out to the street.

Stroker made his way over to Big Dave who shooed Dude off, and they gave each other a big hug and slaps on the backs. That's where I wanted to be with the club members. The kind of loyalty the Noblemen had to each other was rarely found in outsiders. These guys were real, and they would die for each other. That's what I was going through all this shit for—to be a part of the brotherhood.

Stroker and Big Dave talked for a minute, before signaling Dude to come back over. Stroker threw his arm over Dude's shoulder and pulled him in close. I couldn't hear what he said to him, but Dude smiled and slapped Stroker on the back before walking away again.

Well that sure as shit seemed more cordial than my conversation with him, I thought irritated. It was becoming only too clear that I was the underdog tonight. But then again, I kind of liked the idea of being an underdog; it lit a fire under my ass to beat the hell out of Dude. I was ready now more than ever. Dude was going to pay for putting my patch on the line; he was going to pay big time.

My adrenaline and anger pumped through me so fast that I couldn't see straight. Now I was aching to get started. I paced a bit to try and calm down, but I was too pumped.

Someone shouted my name from across the yard, and I spun around. It was Hiney, and he was waving for me to come over.

I made my way through the crowded yard and up to where he was standing. "I told Huey how you waited out at the dam for over 12 hours in the cold," he said. "I also told him how you said you were going to stay until they arrived, no matter how long it took."

"What'd he say?" I asked.

He grinned. "Huey was happy you passed the test. He said that was enough to clear you for now. You don't have to prove anything tonight. It's up to Big Dave to square things away with Huey on Dude's attitude with Baron."

I didn't know if I was relieved or annoyed. "Man, I know I'm just a prospect, but I don't need you to protect me. I need to prove to everyone that I have what it takes to wear a full patch."

"Oh, and you think kicking a prospect's ass will prove you're worthy?"

"Isn't that what the club does when two members have a problem? They take it out back and duke it out."

"That's right, asshole!" Hiney yelled. "The key word here is 'members.' You don't have that privilege as a prospect."

"But I thought everyone here was expecting a fight tonight. Even Stroker came up to me and said this was the night that will either make or break me."

He sighed. "Members will say and do anything to get you rattled. I shouldn't be telling you this, but it's mostly a mind game to make or break you."

"Well it's working, but I'm still pissed at Dude. He ratted me out to Stroker, and I hate that."

"All I can tell you, Turk, is to leave the club out of it. You hear me?" His voice was slowly rising again. "The club doesn't want to hear about anymore shit from you or Dude. You two are just prospects, and the club has bigger issues to worry about than two low-life prospects. It's fucking over!"

I looked across the yard to where Big Dave and Dude where standing and shook my head in disgust. I knew in my heart it wasn't over. I stared at Dude until he looked up at me. I made sure my expression alone made it quite clear how mad I was. He glared back and took a step towards me.

"You got a fucking problem?" he yelled.

"You're damn right I do," I spat back. "What're you going to do about it?"

Big Dave threw his arm out against Dude's chest, stopping him in his tracks. Dude held his ground, and Big Dave stuck his finger in his face.

"Don't fucking move!" Dave yelled. He turned and yelled over to me, "Prospect, get your ass over here!"

As I walked over, I wondered what kind of trouble my big mouth had gotten me into now.

"Do you actually think you could through a temper tantrum in front of the club and get away with it?" he yelled. Dave grabbed both of us by the backs of our necks like we were two newborn kittens and continued his lecture. "You guys are just low-life shit to us. From now on, you two keep your damn mouths shut at club meetings unless spoken to. Got it?"

"I got it, Dave," answered Dude.

My anger was still running hot through my veins, so instead of talking and screwing myself over, I just nodded in agreement and stared at Dude.

"I don't think you're feeling what I'm saying Turk." He leaned in and pushed his face into mine. "I'm thinking that maybe you need to prove to me that I'm not going to have a problem with you."

I swallowed my pride and said, "Hey man, I'm sorry. I respect you, Dave, and I'm on board with anything you say."

I sure as hell didn't want to make enemies with any of the patches. My temper would be my downfall with this club if I didn't learn how to control it quickly. I looked around and saw the members starting to make their way into the clubhouse.

"That's good to hear, Turk," Dave said with narrowed eyes. "Remember, the club doesn't just want more members for the sake of numbers. You need to be an asset to the club. If you two want my vote, you better figure out what it is you two have to bring to the table, or you're gonna be prospects for a long time. Now," he shoved us away from him roughly and said, "go stand your posts."

When the yard finally emptied into the club house, Dude and I were left alone, staring at each other. The silence was broken by the roar of straight pipes. It was Shorty, and he was late.

Dude and I made our way over to him as he was backing his bike up between the others. Shorty yanked off his skid lid and hung it over his mirror.

"Hey guys! Did I miss anything?" Shorty asked cheerfully.

Dude and I yelled, almost simultaneously, "Shut up, Shorty!"

I could hear Shorty's whiny voice say, "What'd I do?" as I walked toward the backyard.

"You're late, asswipe," Dude said. "Baron is pissed."

"Baron's not my sponsor," Shorty replied. "What business is it of his?"

I stopped and turned around. Dude had already stepped over into Shorty's face and stuck his finger into his chest.

"Listen up, you short fuck," Dude barked. "If Baron doesn't kick your ass for that, I will."

Shorty slapped his hand away and puts his finger into Dude's chest.

"You're going to feel real stupid when my short ass beats your fat ass."

"If you two keep yelling, the whole club will be out here in two seconds, and they'll kick all our asses," I said, having made my way back to where they were snarling at each other. I turned to Dude; the shit between us needed to end.

"You know what, Dude? You and I need to cool it until we find out what the club wants to do with us. My patch means a whole lot more than arguing with you, and I'm sure you feel the same."

His brows softened just slightly. "Yeah, you're right. We have a long road ahead of us, and being at odds isn't making any of this easier."

I smiled, and though he obviously tried not to, Dude finally had to smile. We hugged and gave each other hard back slaps. We were all under a lot of stress, and biting each other's heads off was just a product of the strain of prospecting.

We stood our posts for the rest of the night without saying too much to each other. There seemed to be a kind of a dark cloud hanging over us as we waited for the meeting to end. Something told the both of us that things weren't quite over with this affair as far as the club was concerned.

A roar of laughter erupted inside the house, telling us that the meeting was finally over. The three of us gathered in the front yard to greet the members as they came out. Only about four or five members had made their way to the front yard before Baron burst outside yelling.

"Where's that low-life son of a bitch?!"

Honestly, nobody knew for sure which of us he was talking about. I braced myself for an ass-chewing—it was reasonable to assume I'd done something to piss him off—but his eyes fell on Shorty.

Thank God, I thought. For once it wasn't me.

Shorty just stood frozen in fear. Fury flashed in Baron's eyes as he headed towards where Shorty stood practically quivering. As Baron closed the gap between them, Shorty braced for the impact. As soon as he was within arm's reach, Baron shoved him with all his might, sending Shorty down on his ass. Before he could get up, Baron was towering over him.

"Why were you late for the meeting tonight, asshole?" Baron shouted. "Were you too busy doing a drug deal?"

"Are you fucking kidding me?" Shorty sputtered in disbelief. By this point, the other members had converged and were snickering at the display.

Shorty pushed himself up to his feet in a hopeless attempt to regain some dignity. "No, man!" he said, brushing the dirt off his seat but keeping his eyes locked on Baron. "I just had my head up my ass tonight, I guess. It won't happen again."

Baron's eyes narrowed viciously. "How much shit do you have on you tonight, you fucking worm? And don't even *think* about bullshitting me!" It was no secret that Shorty sold weed and that he was always carrying.

Shorty nervously patted around his vest, forgetting in his fear which pocket held his stash. "Just a dime bag. Honest! Do you want me to roll you a couple?"

"No," Baron smiled greedily. "The dime bag will do just fine."

"What?" The terrified expression dropped from Shorty's face, replaced by one of an idiot's confusion. "What do you mean?"

"Your fine for being late to the club meeting is your dime bag. Hand it over."

Obviously annoyed by the turn of events but backed into a corner, Shorty slowly reached into his inner vest pocket and pulled out the dusty baggy. Baron snatched it from his hand and raised it in the air over his head like a trophy.

"Now we have party material, boys!" he yelled like a victory cheer. "Who'd like to join me on this joint venture?"

Several guys came over immediately and slapped Baron on the back before following him back inside. Big Dave and Hiney came out just before the whooping group closed the door. They stopped in the middle of the yard, exchanged a few words, then walked over to where the three of us stood—two laughing, the other scratching his head and wondering what the hell just happened. The laughter stopped as we saw their expressions. They looked the way I'd seen a judge look just before handing down a sentence.

"I'm only going to explain this once to you prospects," Big Dave said, crossing his arms. "The club has decided that it doesn't want any new members that are unstable mental cases. And right now the three of you fall into that category. So the next time—and I mean the *very* next time—any of you cross the line, it's over."

"Let me help Dave clarify what we mean by 'it's over,'" Hiney chimed in. "At the minimum, you go to the hospital, but I'm thinking more like the morgue."

"And God help you if you think we're kidding," said Dave. His fists were clinched tightly as if he were holding back from hitting us. "This is the last time we're sticking our necks out for you prospects."

"Now the three of you get your asses on your sleds," Hiney said. "To-night's not over yet."

The three of us hightailed it to our scoots like hell was on our heels. I started my bike and pulled my helmet on. Hiney and Big Dave pulled out, and my Harley clunked into first as I followed behind them. Each ride with the members was a lesson in reckless driving. We tore through traffic, passed cars on the shoulders, ran stop signs, drove into oncoming traffic, and slipped between cars just for the hell of it.

After another adrenaline-fueled ride, we arrived at the Backstreet Tavern and backed our bikes in.

"Shorty, you're with us," Dave yelled before he and Hiney strode through the door.

That left Dude and me outside to watch the bikes and monitor the parking lot for unwelcome activity. I looked over at Dude and had to smile.

"Deja vu," I chuckled. "If another car pulls into this lot, I'll let you have them."

Cracking a smile himself, Dude said, "Now that I look back on it I have to admit, it was all really stupid. Did you ever see those girls again?"

"Yeah, I hooked up with them later that night," I grinned. "May be taking a trip to California to visit one of them sometime soon, too. Jody, the driver, seems like a pretty cool chick."

"I better go with you and make sure you don't go and fall in love." He was just shooting the piss, but I agreed.

"You know what? That actually sounds like a good idea," I said. "We need to start making some plans for a road trip."

"Quit dreaming, Turk," Dude said, leaning back against his bike. "We're not going anywhere while we're still prospects. The club owns us right now."

He was right. I lowered my head and nodded. We surrendered our souls to the club when we put on our prospect patches. The club came first, and your whole life was focused on what the club needed. I knew there would be sacrifices, and I was good with that.

"Eh, you can't blame a man for dreaming." I shrugged. "It's all we have right now to keep us sane."

CHAPTER 7

DAY OFF

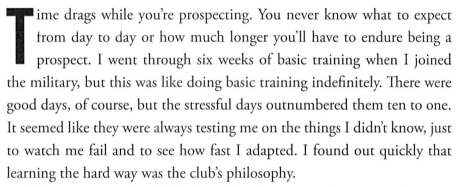

Time drags while you're prospecting. You never know what to expect from day to day or how much longer you'll have to endure being a prospect. I went through six weeks of basic training when I joined the military, but this was like doing basic training indefinitely. There were good days, of course, but the stressful days outnumbered them ten to one. It seemed like they were always testing me on the things I didn't know, just to watch me fail and to see how fast I adapted. I found out quickly that learning the hard way was the club's philosophy.

The occasions when I'd find myself without some duty or another were rare, but one night, I found myself with a night off. I had checked in with Hiney, and he confirmed that he didn't need me that night. Then I contacted the officers—Baby Huey, Doc, and Stroker—,and they all said to just check back with them in the morning. That was all I needed to hear, the night was mine.

I felt almost guilty, not hanging with the patches, but I needed a night to clear my head. It was almost hard to figure out what I was going to do with all my free time. My first thought was to go somewhere no one knew me and have a drink.

I headed for a bar on Western Avenue called The Hob Nob. I'd seen the bar as I passed by it but never had the opportunity to stop in. I wanted to try a place where I knew I'd be anonymous, and this spot was as good as any.

Now, I love older bars, but this place was a dump by anyone's standards. But it had a badass rock and roll band playing, so I figured I'd give it a shot. I walked in past the bouncer, who never gave me a second look, and had to smile. If I'd had on my club colors, it definitely wouldn't have been so easy to walk right in. Non-biker bars always think we're out to cause trouble.

After a quick perusal of the options, I made my way over to the crowded bar and snuggled between two nice looking young ladies. They looked at me and smiled, or perhaps it was a smirk. I wasn't sure, but I didn't care.

"How are you ladies doing tonight?"

After a short moment of silence, the girl on my left walked around me to the other side of her friend and resumed their conversation like I hadn't even spoken.

So it was definitely a smirk. Oh well, I thought. *The night is young.*

I finally caught the bartender's attention after a few minutes and ordered my Jack and coke. He turned without a word and grabbed a well bourbon from the speed rack, pouring it into the coke.

With a slosh, he set the drink down and shouted above the band, "$5.50, bud!"

I narrowed my eyes. "That's not what I asked for."

"Uh, yes sir, it is." He seemed genuinely confused. "Is there a problem?"

I sighed. So many assholes and so little time. I had to decide if it was worth it to start my night off on a bad note.

"Well, you're charging me for a Jack Daniels and coke, but serving me house bourbon and coke. That's the problem. I'll drink it, but don't you think you should charge me accordingly?"

"Look, guy, all mixed drinks are $5.50 when the band is playing. Come on, I'm busy!" He held out his hand, demanding payment.

It's what I get for dressing like a citizen. I smiled and slid him a tenner. "I want my change—all of it."

With a sneer, he turned to the register. After unceremoniously smacking my change down in front of me, he said, "You know, *pal,* 'tips' stands for 'To Insure Prompt Service.' Good luck getting another drink."

Any other night, I probably would have slugged him or at least started some shit, but there were other bartenders, and I really wanted to just enjoy myself. I grabbed my highball and turned to check out the crowd. Most of the women seemed to have dates, but there were a few tables of girls sitting together without men around. It looked like there was plenty of competition over at the bar, but it didn't look tough.

I found a payphone and checked in with Hiney. I wanted to make sure nothing went down without me. Hell, it was the weekend—anything could happen at any time.

The band was rocking when I hung up. After a few more drinks—the other bartender seemed to comprehend the words "Jack and coke"—I was ready to dance. I made my way over to a table I had been watching with three ladies sitting alone, enjoying themselves.

"You know, I'm having a very hard time making a decision about something, so I was hoping you ladies could help me out," I said.

Obviously seeing straight through my come-on, one rolled her eyes, another took a long sip of her drink, and the third looked around the room for someone to save them. I squatted down beside the table, bringing me about eye level with the girls. *Well, that didn't work,* I thought. *Hell, why not do the unexpected?*

"I'm just curious which one of you is going to turn my offer for a dance down first."

That got their attention. The look on their faces was better than I had anticipated. All three of the ladies were now staring at me. It took a second for them to shake the surprise, but then the one closest to me leaned over and whispered in my ear.

"Nice try, but no cigar."

"No more phone calls, folks, I think we have a winner!" I looked over at the other two. "Do I have a runner up?"

"I'm not ready to dance yet," said the second girl.

Well, that wasn't quite *a rejection.* "How about I buy the next round? You know, to help boost your spirits."

The third finally said, "No, I think we're all right."

"I'll have one!" the second lady blurted out.

Bingo.

Her friends flashed her a dirty look, but she just smiled at them and turned back to me.

"I'll have a Tom Collins."

"Coming right up, ma'am." I stood up and looked at the other two. "Oh, come on, free drinks! What are you two having?"

The second girl sighed and said, "Okay. I'll have a gimlet, and this one wants a Coors Light. And since you're being so generous, how about three shots of Sambuca?"

"Sounds like a plan, girls!"

As I walked away, Coors Light called out, "And don't forget the coffee beans!"

Coffee beans? What the fuck does that mean?

When I reached the bar, I asked the waitress for a pen and a cocktail napkin.

I wrote: "Coffee beans? Nice try, but no cigar." I handed the note to the waitress and gave her a couple bucks to deliver it. They were trying to make a fool out of me, and it put a bad taste in my mouth. As the waitress handed the girls the note and they passed it around, I thought about finishing my drink and finding another bar.

Gimlet and Coors Light covered their mouths as if they were trying not to laugh. Tom Collins was the last to read the note. She looked up at me and shook her head apologetically. She asked the waitress for her pen and turned the napkin over, scribbly furiously. She handed the pen back to the waitress and slid out of her chair. Folding the note into the palm of her hand, she started walking towards me.

I took a large sip of my Jack and coke, hoping for some liquid courage. *What could she possibly have to say?*

When she reached me, she smiled shyly. “I want to apologize for me and my friends,” she said. “We’ve been kind of rude.”

Damn, she’s cute. “That’s all right, I recover quickly.”

“Sambuca can be served with a few coffee beans, but that’s more of an upscale cocktail bar sorta thing.”

“Huh.” I grinned a bit. “Ya learn something new every day.”

She slid the folded note into my shirt pocket with a smile, then went back to her friends. I turned toward the bar and retrieved the note.

“I’ll take that dance whenever you are ready—Liz.”

I refolded the napkin and put it back in my shirt pocket. The night was finally taking a turn for the better. I was ready to dance, but first I needed to make a pit stop. I downed the dregs of my drink and headed for the restroom.

As I stood at the urinal staring at the wall stained with marker signatures of the many losers that patronized this dump, I realized that Liz was right. This bar was definitely not a coffee bean kind of joint.

As I made my way through the crowd to where the girls were sitting, I noticed that the mood at the table had dropped a bit.

“How about that dance?” I asked, kneeling next to Liz.

She turned and said, “I don’t think that’s such a good idea right now.”

“Why, what’s up?” Something was definitely off. The other two girls looked pale.

“Sheri’s ex-boyfriend just showed up,” she said, nodding toward Gimlet. “He just came over to our table and said, ‘I hope you girls aren’t planning on having a good time tonight.’ He’s been a real asshole since Sheri broke up with him. He’s just looking for trouble tonight.”

"Well why don't you let me get you out on the dance floor and help you relax?" I put my hand gently on her bare knee.

She put her hand on top of mine, saying, "I'm sorry. I really do want to dance with you." She looked genuinely disappointed to my surprise.

"Where is the guy now?"

"He's the one in the blue shirt at the bar talking to the guy in white." She squeezed my hand tightly. "Please don't get in trouble on our account."

I leaned forward and kissed her hand, then slowly let go of it. "Don't worry. I'll be right back. This is what I do."

I could feel the girls' eyes boring into my back as I walked toward the bar. *I guess my life just isn't about relaxing. I'm just trouble, looking for a place to happen.*

Sheri's ex-boyfriend must have seen me talking to Liz and didn't seem too happy about it. The creep was keeping a close eye on me as I came up to him. I wanted nothing more than to just walk up and knock him out, but that would have just gotten me thrown out of the bar. Instead I figured I'd just let him set the pace of the conversation. I pretended to ignore him as I took the spot beside him and signaled for the bartender.

Of course, the shit-head bartender from earlier was the closest one. He looked up, saw me, shook his head, and went back to cleaning glasses. The other bartender was busy at the other end of the island, so I quickly rethought my game plan.

"Excuse me, bartender, when you get a chance…" I waved a $5 bill. "I think I forgot to give you something last time."

With a stern frown, he wiped his hands with a bar towel and walked over. He took the five, tapped it twice on the bar, and stuck it in the tip jar behind him.

"What was your problem earlier?" he asked in a less unfriendly tone than I'd expected.

"Sorry, I was sober." I laughed. "How about two Jack and cokes and a shot of Crown?"

"All right, we'll see how you handle this round," he said with a slight smile.

When the drinks were made and set on the bar in front of me, he said, "That'll be $14."

I forked over $25 and told him to keep it. He smiled, eyeballing the bills. It was an expensive round but I figured I'd need a friend if this all went south.

"By the way, the drinks are for these two guys," I said, nodding to my right.

As the drinks were slid in front of them, the guys perked up in surprise. Sheri's ex-boyfriend didn't look too pleased with the offer.

"What are these for?" he asked suspiciously.

"I think everyone here should be having a good time, and you two look like you could use a drink," I said as innocently as I could. I threw back my shot of Crown without taking my eyes off them. "Oh, and I want to dance with Liz. Is that going to be a problem?"

He turned to his drink, obviously relieved to discover that she was the one I wanted. "No, I don't give a shit about Liz. Fuck her brains out for all I care," he said lazily before taking a sip.

I'm not sure what pissed me off more, the tone of his voice or what he'd said.

I tried to swallow the bitter taste in my mouth. "Cool, cool. After that, I think I'll dance with Sheri. She's got a nice ass."

The dude's face went beet-red, and he squeezed the highball glass so tight that it shattered in his hand, sending Jack and coke flying. For a moment, I forgot myself and was impressed—I had never seen that done before.

"You stay away from Sheri, you fucking asshole!" he shouted, pointing his bleeding, glass-crusted finger in my face. "She's my girl! You stay the hell away from her!"

"Am I supposed to be scared of you? Maybe go running from the bar crying?"

"If you know what's good for you, you'll do just that."

The sound of shattered glass and shouting sent the bartender over. "What's the problem, guys?"

"This motherfucker is trying to pick up my girlfriend, and I won't have it," he flung a finger toward me accusingly.

The bartender followed the wagging finger and looked at me, his stern face turning to one of shock.

"Hey, man, go to the restroom."

"What?" That hadn't been what I'd expected to hear.

"Just go to the restroom. Trust me." The bartender looked sick. "I'll handle this."

Whatever, I thought, heading to the bathroom. I shoved the door open, sending it slamming against the wall. I looked into the mirror to see blood splattered all over my face from that asshole's bleeding hand. He had deliberately flicked blood on me while shaking his finger in my face. Fury turned my vision red. He was a dead man.

I splashed water on my face and scrubbed his sickening blood off with a paper towel. All I could think about was getting back out there before they threw the prick out. I wanted to personally see to it that this guy was in pain for a very long time.

My first thought was that he was disrespecting the club. It was my duty to make him pay for it. But, as I took one more quick look in the mirror, I realized that I wasn't wearing my prospect patch. He had no idea I was with the club, but I decided that I was still going to beat his ass for my own gratification.

As I pushed through the restroom door and headed for the bar, Liz was the furthest thing from my mind. My anger had put her to the side for the moment. I scanned the bar for the disrespectful asshole but didn't see him, which only infuriated me more. I wasn't in the restroom that long. Had the coward really turned tail?

I pushed my way through the crowd to the front door. I faintly heard the bartender yelling for me to come back, but I had tunnel vision. I pushed past the two bouncers and found myself in the middle of the parking lot. I thought I had lost him until I heard the squeal of tires. I knew it was him, and my blood started boiling again. He floored the piece of shit he called a car straight at me. I stepped out of his path easily, and as he pulled up next to me with his buddy in the passenger seat, he yelled out the window, "Fuck you, asshole!"

Unfortunately for him, he underestimated just how crazy I was. I leapt through the window and grabbed the steering wheel. He floored it and my right side slammed against the doorframe. I tried to reach for his keys to shut the motor down, but he jerked the wheel to the right. We bounced out into the street, and he floored it again. I wasn't going on this death ride he had planned for me,. so with all my strength, I forced the wheel into a hard right, and we veered onto the sidewalk. I saw a light pole coming up fast, so I pushed myself away from the car and fell to the curb, sliding on my ass and back.

He slammed on his brakes, not soon enough to avoid the pole. I could hear the two jerks yelling profanity as I laid in the street on my back. I got up and started limping in their direction, but suddenly, I was grabbed from behind by two big guys and was being pulled back towards the bar.

"Okay, big guy," said one of the bouncers. "I think you've done enough damage for one night."

"I'm just getting started!" I yelled. "Get off me!"

"Look, asshole. The cops are on their way, and unless you want to face a bunch of charges for forcing that car off the road, I'd suggest you take the rest of the night off."

I looked over at the car and saw the light pole mounted into the grill like a new hood ornament and smiled. The driver was trying to get his door open, but it was too damaged. Satisfaction and pain was building in me as the adrenaline ebbed—I'd hit the road pretty hard.

I patted the two bouncers on their shoulders and thanked them for pulling me out of the street. I told them that they were right and I should call it a night. I climbed in my car and pulled the folded napkin out of my pocket, rereading it.

"I'll take that dance whenever you are ready—Liz."

For a moment, I thought about going back inside, but the approaching red and blue flashing lights told me that it was time to go.

I pulled out into the street just in time to see the driver fumbling as he tried to climb out of his window with the cop looking on. I smiled as I drove away, trying to find a comfortable position in my seat, so my ass and back wouldn't ache so bad.

It was just before midnight when I pulled up in front of my house. I pulled the garage door open and stared at my Harley. The night was still young, and a ride sounded good. I started my bike and relaxed behind the handlebars, thinking that I should have just done this in the first place.

1973

CHAPTER 8

BARON'S WISDOM

It had been a long nine months since I had started prospecting for the club, and I was mentally and physically worn out. It was getting to the point where I didn't want to go out in public anymore. When I did, I usually ended up taking out my frustrations with the club on some poor unsuspecting soul. My tolerance was at an all-time low for people, and I knew it.

I had to keep reminding myself that I was building a life with the club and not interviewing for a job. You can't rush these things, and I was beginning to realize that I needed to slow down and take things on a day-to-day basis. If I didn't start thinking straight and doing things right, I wasn't going to make it. I wanted to patch over so bad I could almost taste it. I knew I was just as good as any member, yet they continued to treat me like I was their property. I knew that once I patched over, I would finally be accepted as a true brother, but until then, the members worked me to the bone.

I don't care how tough you think you are, prospecting will wear at your very soul. I guess that's what I'd signed up for—the long haul, no matter how long.

When I woke up, I sat up and threw my feet over the edge of the bed and just stared at the phone, waiting for it to ring. I hadn't really cleaned my place in a while, and even I was getting a little disgusted with it. The club had me so busy and worn out that the only time I was home was to crash. The place looked like shit, but I didn't care right now. It was the weekend, and even if I didn't get a call, I still had to get my ass over to the club house.

I was in the middle of a long hot shower, which had become the only time I had to relax, when the phone rang.

"Fuck!" I screamed.

As I climbed out, I slammed the shower door so hard that, for a moment, I was worried it would shatter. I grabbed a towel and trod toward the screeching phone, trying to subdue my anger; snapping at a member would only make my life even more hellish.

"Hey," I said, looking down the hall at the trail of wet footprints on the hardwood floor.

"Hi, is this Rick?" a soft womanly voice asked.

That took me by surprise. "Yes, who's this?"

"Hi, Rick. It's Jackie. Remember me?"

"Jackie? Damn, girl, it's been a long time." I hadn't talked to Jackie since the night her father had chased me out of the house at gunpoint for bringing his (unbeknown to me) 17-year-old daughter home so late. She had left to stay with her mom in Utah, and that had been the last I'd heard from her.

"Yes, it has," she admitted. "It took some doing to find you. Everyone I talked to said you dropped off the face of the earth."

"I know," I said with a laugh. "I understand why they would say that."

"Well, I finally convinced one of your coworkers at the Mint to give me your number." She paused. "So, how come you didn't try to contact me?"

"Well, for one thing, you weren't even 18 the last time we saw each other, and it just didn't seem like a good idea to look you up after your father chased us out of the house with a shotgun."

"Yeah, I know." She giggled. "I hadn't had that much excitement in my life since I left for Utah that night. I'll never forget speeding away with you on your Harley."

"Yeah, but that Harley is long gone now. It was stolen," I said, the long-held bitterness creeping into my voice. I forced it back. "I have another bike now, and I like it a lot more anyway. I don't have to kick start this one."

"That's good!" she said. "So, I'm in town. And before you ask, no, I'm not staying at my dad's. And in case you're wondering, I'm 19 now. How about you come pick me up and take me for a ride?"

I didn't need a woman—and especially not a teenager—to complicate my life right now. I was on a journey I had to travel alone, and I sure as hell didn't need any distractions. But her voice brought back memories I had put behind me, and I would have really loved to see her again. Just the thought of her gorgeous blond hair blowing in the wind on the back of my scoot made me ache, but I would just be stirring up a hornet's nest. I was on a short leash with the club. I barely had enough time to shower, much less to devote to a good relationship.

"Look Jackie," I made myself say, "I can't today. But how long are you in town?"

"I know what you're doing Rick," she said. "You think you're too old for me, right? Well, did you forget about all the fun we had that night before you knew how old I was? Riding on the back of your Harley was something I've never forgotten. And that way you kissed me—"

"Jackie!" I cut in. "Slow down! I'm not trying to ditch you, but I can't talk right now. Give me your number, and I'll call you as soon as I can."

"You know what, Rick? Forget it. I can take the hint," she said angrily. "Don't worry about it. I knew this would be a mistake."

"That's not fair, Jackie!" I said. "You have no idea what's happening in my life right now. This new venture I've been working on has kept me really busy, but if everything pans out, I'll be on easy street."

There was a beat of silence on the other end while she considered. "If that's true, then call me on Monday at Lisa's. I'll be in town until Wednesday."

"Okay, cool," I said, relieved. "I can do that."

If she still lived in Utah with her mom, that'd be even better. A long-distance relationship might actually be manageable. I took down Lisa's information and promised to call before hanging up.

While getting dressed, I asked myself about why I was leading on a 19-year-old girl. I knew I was just going to make another problem for myself. The only relationship I needed to have at the moment was with the club, but I just couldn't help myself when it came to Jackie.

I still hadn't heard from the guys, so I figured I'd better head over to the clubhouse. I hopped onto my '72 Sportster and sped off. As I drove, my thoughts turned, again, to Jackie. I was bummed, thinking about how much I wished I could go out with her like any normal person could have. I knew the club was supposed to be the first and only thing on my mind, but I was 24, and I wanted it all.

When the clubhouse came into view, I felt an unexpected wave of depression flow through my body. I kicked down through the gears and pulled in. Maneuvering past the potholes and rocks of the desert driveway pretty much required the skill of a stuntman. There were only two bikes out front: Baby Huey's and Baron's.

I got to the front door and paused.

Why the hell am I even here? I asked myself. *Does the club even know what I'm going through? Would they care?*

I pounded on the door and heard a shout from inside. "Get in here, Turk!"

I pushed open the door and walked blindly into the darkness of the living room. It took a few seconds for my eyes to adjust from the midday desert sun. All the curtains had been pulled shut and the television was the only light in the room.

"Why are you sitting in the dark?" I asked, squinting at Baby Huey.

"It makes the place look much cleaner. Why do you think?"

I smiled at his sarcasm and made my way over to the other end of the couch where I slumped down before jumping as a spring bit me in the ass.

"Hey, Huey," I said, repositioning myself. "What's the plan for today?"

"No plans, Turk," he said genially. "But that could change at any second."

I leaned back into the couch and tried to settle in for what I figured would be another long, boring day. The cheerful sounds of Sesame Street drifted over to where I sat from the tube. I smiled weakly as my eyes drifted upward to the ceiling. I knew that if I closed them, I would lose consciousness. For a brief moment, Jackie's smile came back into my head. I needed to touch someone soft soon, or I was going to lose my mind.

I was just about to give in and let my body slide into a sweet dream about Jackie when the back door crashed open, sending me practically through the roof.

"I can't see shit in this place!" Baron's voice boomed from the doorway. "Open a curtain in here or something."

"Did you just come in here to bitch, or do you need something?" Huey snapped, obviously irritated at having his wholesome educational program interrupted.

Baron stared at me, just realizing I was there. I couldn't make out his expression because the sun was to his back, but somehow, I knew I was getting the famous Baron stare. "Goddamn, Turk," he yelled. "Why don't you call it quits with the club, so I don't have to look at your ugly mug anymore? Jesus, what's it going to take to get rid of you?"

If only he knew how close I was to doing just that. But my hatred of being told what to do won out.

"Nothing short of death will make me quit, Baron!" I said, infusing my voice with a good heaping dose of false cheeriness.

"Well," he replied with a smirk, "this is going to be easier than I thought then."

That was it. Baron had just stepped on my last nerve. I pushed myself up and got in his face.

"You want me dead? Go ahead and do me," I said. When he didn't respond, I got even closer to him and yelled again. "Do it! I'm right here!"

With a quick jerk, Baron pulled the blade from his belt and brought it up under my neck. He grabbed my throat with his other hand and with the force of a lineman, shoved me against the wall behind the front door. The door slammed shut, and darkness fell again on the room.

I was blinded momentarily, but I could smell the stale vodka on Baron's breath as he pushed his weight against me, keeping me pinned to the wall. His grip around my throat tightened as he spoke.

"You fucking low-life prospect! You have the nerve to challenge me? I oughta gut you right here and now!"

The sharp edge of the knife kissed the skin of my throat, and I felt a trickle of blood race down my neck. Maybe Baron was right. I was exhausted from the daily beatdowns and constant derision. Maybe I did need to move on with my life.

Suddenly, the knife was removed from my throat, and Baron's elbow cracked across my forehead. No sooner had I straightened back up than the knife was back at my throat.

"Well, shithead," Baron yelled, flinging spittle into my face. "Where do you want to go from here? The way I see it, you have two options. You can hand me your prospect cut and walk out the front door or be carried out the back door."

"Baron!" Baby Huey yelled from where he still lounged on the couch. "Do what you have to do, but if you stick Turk in the living room, you're cleaning the mess up yourself."

"Just keep the curtains drawn, and no one will notice the mess," I said casually.

Baby Huey bust out laughing, and Baron slowly pulled the knife from my throat. "Damn, Turk, you're sick," he said. "You really think this is a time to joke?"

"I just don't have my shit together today," I said. "You guys make me feel like my whole life is a joke."

"Oh, boo hoo. I really do want to cut your throat now. Next thing you know, you're going be curled up crying."

"I'm not ready to be gutted just yet, if that's all right, Baron."

"Be warned, Turk," Baron said darkly. "If you ever get in my face again—"

"I know, Baron. I was wrong. I should've never challenged you. I had a temporary lapse. My head's not on straight today." I slowly slid down the wall and put my hands behind my head. *What the fuck am I doing?* I thought. *I need to get the hell out of here. I just went off on Baron—what was I thinking? That's a good way to get killed. Or worse, tossed out.* "I don't know, Baron," I said. "Everything just seems to be getting harder."

Baron thought for a moment, then knelt down and put a finger into my chest. "Listen to me, Turk," he said. His softer tone threw me off. I looked up at him as he said, "The closer to the top of the mountain you get, the harder the wind blows."

That hit me like a ton of bricks. Had that really just come out of *Baron's* mouth? Suddenly, it all made sense. *I'm close to the summit. He just said so himself...* "Thanks, man," I managed to finally say.

He stood up and held his hand out to me. I grabbed it and he pulled me up.

"Keep it together, Turk," Baron said. "You're doing just fine." I just smiled. "Now," he said, his gruff tone returning, "get your ass down to Cecil's Custom Cycle Shop and pick up a 6-volt regulator for me. Cecil knows my bike, so he'll know what you're talking about. Here's $10, and I want my change."

I turned and opened the front door, but hesitated a moment. I looked back at Baron and thought about thanking him again for his words of confidence, but that thought ended abruptly as Huey yelled at me.

"Shut the goddamn door, Turk! You're letting all the dark out."

I smiled and stepped out into the morning sunlight. *These guys are already my brothers,* I thought. *I'm just still the little brother for now.*

1974

CHAPTER 9

PATCHED

I hung on to what Baron had said to me that weekend when I was about ready to give up. Baron's words made it clear to me that the only limitations you have are the ones you put on yourself. I felt stronger than ever before because of his words, and I was willing to go the extra mile to achieve what I wanted done.

When the Wednesday night meeting ended, it was time for the members to relax at a well-known local watering hole. We were all at Thud Puckers Pub late that night, and I was just starting to relax. Three prospects were outside watching the bikes and monitoring everyone who drove up. I was inside with the patches as they sat in a corner booth overlooking the bar and the front door. A couple of tattooed independents (dudes who didn't ride with a club but rode just as hard) were eyeballing us from the bar. I could see they were real drunk and cocky. I was keeping an eye on them too, and they knew it.

After a few minutes, they got up and started walking our way. One walked right up and got so close to my face that I could smell the whiskey on his breath.

"Hey, man, just thought we'd come over and pay our respects."

I put my finger to his throat and pushed him and his stinking ass-breath back. That's when I noticed that the second guy had slipped by me and sat down in the booth beside the patches. Before he had a chance to say a word, I was in his face.

"Dude!" I yelled. "Stand the fuck up—now!"

"Hey man," said the tattooed stranger. "What's your problem?"

I never repeated myself. I reached down, put him in a chokehold, and pulled his ass out of the booth. I swung him around and threw him into his buddy.

"Nobody invited you to sit down," I said. "Now get the fuck out of here."

They walked back over to their stools and sat down. I looked back over at the patches to see if they had anything to say about what just happened.

"Next time they come over here," Huey said. "I want you to kick their asses."

"It'll be my pleasure," I said.

"That's what I thought," he said with a smile.

The dudes at the bar had started whispering to each other, and that was really pissing me off. Baby Huey was watching them too and nodded to me in their direction. I walked over and confronted the two independents.

"When I said 'Get the fuck out of here,' I meant get the fuck out of here!"

"What?" one said dumbly. "You trying to tell us we have to leave?"

There they go again, trying to make me repeat myself. I slapped him hard upside the head, sending him sliding off the bar stool, staggering.

"What the fuck do you think now?"

I followed them out the front door and nodded to the three prospects by the bikes. The two dudes climbed onto their bikes and started putting their helmets on. The four of us circled their bikes. They stopped what they were doing and looked at each other.

"You gonna let us leave, or what?"

I narrowed my eyes. "How about we go with 'or what.'"

Punches flew and soon the punks were on the ground, pinned under their bikes. They were lucky we were just trying to make a point and not actually out for blood. We didn't want to hurt them too bad because they needed to ride their bikes out of there.

"I'm going back inside to report to Huey," I said to the other prospects as they chuckled at the bikers struggling with the weight pinning them down. "Make sure they leave before we come out."

"Sure thing," Shorty said. "We got them."

I looked at my bros and smiled before returning inside to my place beside the booth. When Huey looked up, I punched my fist into my open hand. He nodded and smiled.

"Go get a couple shots of Jack, Turk," Huey said.

I ordered them up and set them down in front of him. He grabbed one and slid the other towards me. I was caught off guard somewhat, because prospects were not allowed to drink while out with patches. Baby Huey saw my expression and pointed to the shot in front of me.

"That's for you," Huey said, his tone not brokering discussion. "Pick it up!"

I grabbed the Jack, saluted Huey, and threw it back.

"That's for taking care of business," Huey said as he slapped me on the back. "I like that about you. I don't have to say a word. You know how to take care of shit when it needs taking care of—no questions asked."

"Well," I said, "I learned from the best."

Huey's praise made me practically glow with pleasure. It made it all worthwhile, and I was more determined than ever to patch over. Not knowing when that'd happen, though, had been very frustrating these past nine months, and it seemed like it was taking an eternity. It was up to your sponsor to call for a vote, and the rules were simple. If one member didn't vote in your favor, the club would hear his reasons why and decide if it was enough to keep you from patching. If two members voted against you, you were sentenced to at least another 6 months before you could come up for vote again. That's why I wanted to know all the members and do whatever they needed done. I couldn't risk those two votes sending me into another half-year of servitude.

Though I tended to doubt myself when it came to the club, I had no trouble handling outsiders. That confidence came from my training in the martial arts. I worked out hard in the dojo for the last four years and had made somewhat of a name for myself in the tournament circuit. In the early days of kickboxing, safety gear was comprised solely of knuckle pads and shin guards. Having your ribs bruised, cracked, or broken was plenty common in our dojo. We trained hard, and it came at a price. If we injured a leg while training, we practiced our hand techniques and vice versa. We learned to work around our injuries to stay at the top of our game—no excuses.

My life with the club never intersected with my life in the dojo. Once I entered the training hall, I emptied my mind of all outside thoughts and focused on my fighting skills. The club knew I trained, but they didn't know where. The dojo was my private sanctuary from everything in the outside world.

Even though I enjoyed teaching classes, tournament kickboxing was what I loved to do. Climbing into the ring with another black belt fed my need for adrenaline. It was how I tested my techniques against other opponents of my skill level. And it was also what gave me the confidence I needed in bad situations with outsiders. How often did the average bar patron practice punching a heavy bag? To throw a good punch, you need to shadow box to gain speed, hit the heavy bag for power, and free-spar to work on timing and focus.

Fighting came naturally to me, which was probably why I fit so well into the lifestyle of a biker club. If they needed something taken care of, I didn't hesitate or ask questions because that's not what you do in the ring.

I was never asked to do anything illegal—that wasn't what the club was about. Sure, not every member was a model citizen, but the club was never party to it.

I wasn't a thief or a liar, but I was Irish, and I loved to fight. Right or wrong, I backed my bros in any situation. The members were aware of my abilities and my total loyalty to the club, which gave me a slight edge over the other prospects.

A few days after the incident at Thud Puckers, I arrived at the weekly meeting spot and joined the other prospects in the front yard. We always tried to keep each others' spirits up since prospecting was such a tough time, and that was especially the case when one of us got laid into.

I was outside with Dude and Shorty and a new prospect, named Lance. We were just shooting the shit when about an hour after the meeting had started, Stroker came outside.

"Hey, Turk, get your ass in here!" he yelled,

I looked at Shorty and Dude and shrugged my shoulders. I figured they just wanted to send me for a beer run or something, so I shouted, "Right behind ya!" and followed him inside.

That was the very first time I entered the living room during a meeting. Everyone was staring at me when I came in, and I realized that I had probably done something wrong and was about to get my ass kicked. Either that or they had something very special for me to do.

Stroker shoved me into the middle of the living room, and Baby Huey stood up.

"I never personally bring a prospect up for vote that I didn't sponsor, but I'm making an exception in your case, Turk," he said. My stomach practically fell out my ass. This was it. "I suggested that we take a vote amongst ourselves to see if you're ready to full patch."

Huey reached down and picked up a paper bag. He smiled and tossed the bag to me. I snatched it out of the air and looked around at everyone before opening the sack and looking inside.

Holy fucking hell…

Prospects wear only the club's bottom rocker patch, which usually just identifies the state or area you're from. The top rocker and center patch are reserved for full-patch members only, and that's what I was looking at.

"The boys have decided you're ready to become one of us," he said, sounding like a proud dad. "That all right with you, Turk?"

"Holy shit! Yeah! *Hell* yeah!"

I felt as light as a feather. All the stress and burdens of being a prospect were gone. I couldn't help myself. I pulled the patches out of the bag and held them over my head and shouted, "I did it, Hiney! I did it!"

With a short laugh, Huey said, "All right, all right. Now, Turk, one of the most important things for you to remember is that now that you have your patches, you can't ever lose them to *anyone.* Got that?"

Before I could respond, everyone stood up as one like Huey had just rung a bell. Almost all of them had devilish smiles as they converged on me and began grabbing at my patches and pulling at me to get to them.

Ah...I see.

Even though I knew what they were doing, I was getting pissed and fighting back hard. They gave me no choice; I didn't dare lose my patches, especially after I'd *just* gotten them. Some of the guys took some hard shots as I flung my elbows. I was being grabbed from all directions. I heard the sickening crunch of someone's nose breaking when I flung my fist up to punch whoever was grasping at my patches just over my shoulder.

At that, Huey had seen enough. He whistled, and the melee ended as quickly as it had begun. The same men who'd been punching me in the kidneys to get my patches just a moment before were now hugging me and slapping me on the back, even Rotten Ralph, whose gnarled nose was pouring blood like a faucet from my punch. Everyone was congratulating me and calling me "brother."

I was in disbelief. Was this really happening? I was so relieved. I was a full patch now, and it was time to party. I held the patches tightly in my hands and couldn't believe how good the material felt beneath my fingertips. I wanted them on my vest that very instant. After he'd called the meeting to an end, Baby Huey's ol'lady, Peggy, walked up to me and held out a tube of fabric glue.

"Lew said you'd be wanting your patches on right away, so I brought this along for you. You can glue them on tonight and get them sewn on tomorrow," she said with a sweet smile. "Congratulations, Turk! You earned it!"

"Thanks, Peggy!"

I headed for the kitchen table, taking my vest off as I went.

"Here," Peggy said, coming up behind me. "Let me do that. I've done my fair share of these, and I know how to make it look right."

I handed her the vest and glue and stood back. "She's all yours. Do you need any help?"

"Get out of here and let me do my magic. Go celebrate!"

She didn't need to tell me twice. It was hard to leave my vest, but I ran back into the living room and jumped on Hiney's back. He swung around, and we both landed on the floor laughing. The celebration had started, and it spilled out into the front yard. We were all fighting and wrestling with each other but a bit more playfully than before. Our club was always ready to party at a moment's notice, and this was the best reason ever.

About a half hour later, Baby Huey walked out of the front door holding my cut-off Levi vest. I went to grab it, but he pulled it back.

I took a step back and everyone got quiet.

"Let me make a few things clear to you, Turk," Huey said solemnly. "Some of these things you should already know."

"Sure, Huey," I said seriously. "I'm listening."

"These colors belong to the club, not you. Is that understood? If you leave the club, the colors stay."

"Ok, and…"

"If you lose these colors, you become an organ donor. Is that clear?"

"Yes, very clear."

"No one fucking else will *ever* wear your colors...no one."

"Gotcha!"

"These colors represent everything we stand for, what happens to these colors reflects on the whole club. Don't even think about disappointing me, Turk. You hear me?"

"I hear you brother—loud and clear. Huey, I'm ready to stand by your side and defend this club with my life if need be."

Baby Huey smiled and tossed the vest to me. I caught it and held it up for everyone to see. I then flipped it around and swung it over my shoulders. I could feel the extra weight of the patches on my back, and it felt good. I turned to all the members in the yard and threw my hands in the air.

"Fuck, I love you guys!"

The party was on. Hiney made his way over to me and pulled me aside.

"It's about fucking time, Turk! Love you, man!" He slapped me on the back and planted a big kiss on the top of my head.

"Thanks, Hiney," I said, laughing. "You know, I owe all this to you. You have supported me since day one, and I will always be indebted to you."

I threw my arm over Hiney's shoulder and looked around at everyone in the yard. Then I spotted him—the one member I swore I'd beat the hell out of as soon as I'd patched. But now Baron was holding his bottle of vodka out for me to take with a huge grin on his face. I had to smile. I grabbed the bottle from him and took a large swallow.

"Now that it's over, what did I teach you?" Baron asked, throwing his arm over my shoulder.

I laughed. "You made me tougher than I ever thought possible, Baron. And I love you for it, even if it made me want to kill you a couple times."

Our hands met in a high five slap, and we came together in a body slam hug. All my negative thoughts toward him were gone. We were brothers now.

I looked over at Hiney and pulled him into a bear hug.

"God, I feel great!" I yelled. "Let's get this party started!"

I was 24 years old and had the world by the balls. How could it get any better? I had a great job at the Mint Hotel as the valet manager; I rode a Harley, and I was finally a member of one of the strongest clubs in Las Vegas. We did whatever we wanted, and there was no one to stop us. What could be better?

I felt sorry for the citizens who spent each day hating their jobs, their lives, and who they were. But it was these same people who would criticize us and put us down because we were different.

We were different because we were free—free to live our lives however we wanted. They hated us because we were what freedom was all about, and they weren't strong enough to claim their share of the good life. In my eyes, they were weak and the pawns of society.

"I need a drink!" I yelled. "Who's with me?"

Hiney pushed me towards my bike and pointed at me. "I've got your first Jack!"

"You're on, man," I said. "Now get your ass on your Harley, and let's ride!"

It was absolutely thrilling. As a prospect, I never would've been allowed to talk to a member that way. I could get use to this life real fast.

I stepped over my '72 Sportster and brought her to life. I sat there with my scoot vibrating between my legs as the other guys started their mills, one by one. The noise got louder and louder as all the engines roared to life. Everyone was yelling and gunning their motors in celebration of my passage into the ranks of the club.

Tonight, it was all about me, and I was loving every minute of it. I actually felt the guys were waiting for this night to vote me in just as much as I was. I may have had a bit of an ego, but the patch on my back gave me that right.

We raced away from the clubhouse and headed for the Backstreet Tavern. I no longer had to ride at the back of the pack, although the front spots were reserved for the officers.

Everything felt different now, from the wind in my hair to the scoot vibrating beneath me and the smell of the night air. I had just patched, and I had to keep pinching myself to believe that it had really happened. I felt the brotherhood so much deeper now because I felt accepted by the group. It was real and no longer a dream. As we rode, I looked at the guys around me and was never prouder of my club, my bros, and my patch.

As we backed our bikes in at the Tavern, Dude and Shorty were already in the bar checking it out. They came running out and nodded the all clear. Everyone filed into the bar except me. I paused a moment because I needed to say something to the prospects.

"Hey guys," I said. "You know I love you two. Hang in there—you're next."

"Right on, Turk!" Dude smiled. "You've really inspired us. To see you patch over gives us hope. Congratulations, man!"

"Yeah, man," Shorty added. "Good for you, Turk. We've got your back so get in there and enjoy your party!"

"Yeah, and have a couple for us!"

We slapped each other's backs, and I went inside to party. I was sick for two days straight afterwards, but I'll never forget that night.

1975

CHAPTER 10

JEN'S INFO

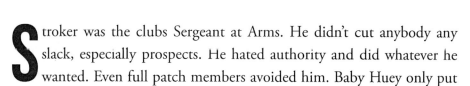

Stroker was the clubs Sergeant at Arms. He didn't cut anybody any slack, especially prospects. He hated authority and did whatever he wanted. Even full patch members avoided him. Baby Huey only put up with Stroker's shit because he got things done. His way might have been a little messy at times, but shit got done never the less.

For me, Stroker was a personal challenge. He didn't scare me, and I made it a point to hang out with him to try and gain his trust. Even though he loved the club, I believed he was a loner at heart, which made him a very hard man to get to know. Whenever I'd find him sitting alone at the bar, I'd go over and start a conversation. His first reaction was usually, "What the hell do you want?" But one day, I finally got to him.

"What's the deal, Turk? Why are you always bothering me?"

"Bothering you? I call it friendly conversation," I said cheerfully.

"I don't need your fucking friendly conversation. Just let me drink my beer, all right?"

"Is that anyway to talk to your best friend?" I went on innocently.

"Turk, I'm warning you. Leave me the fuck alone."

"You know, Stroker, I don't respond well to threats. You should buy me a drink and say you're sorry."

That had done it. He shot up, sending his stool flying behind him. Everyone in the bar was on their feet, waiting for Stroker to knock me on my ass.

"Goddamn it, Turk!" Stroker yelled. "I'm going to kick your ass if you don't get away from me!"

"So, is that my cue to start running?"

"Only if you know what's good for you."

"Stroker," I said calmly, "I'm not going anywhere until you let me buy you a drink."

"If that's what it takes to get rid of you, then order it up!"

I couldn't help myself. "Well, let's just say I'm buying the first round."

Stroker grabbed me by the throat with both hands and started squeezing. I could feel my face getting red as his chokehold got tighter and tighter. I didn't want to fight him, but I was in pain and going to lose consciousness real soon. I reached up and applied pressure to his windpipe with my two fingers in a desperate move, but all I got was a tighter grip around my throat. In a last ditch effort, I slapped the hell out of both his ears at the same time. He grimaced in pain and swung me around, pinning my back to the wall.

I grabbed his throat and returned the choke. As we both stood there, choking the shit out of each other, Huey yelled at the other members to break us up.

We stood apart staring at each other as Huey walked over.

"What the hell is going on with you two?" Huey yelled.

"I was just checking out Turk's karate skills," Stroker said. "I think he needs a little more gym time."

"You're good, Stroker," I said, my voice soundly only a little tight. "Good and strong. Now, let's have that drink, and I'll let you coach me on my fighting abilities."

Stroker smiled and held his hand out. As I went to shake it, he swung it up and slapped me hard on the side of my face.

"That's for choking me so hard," Stroker said.

I had to laugh as I put my hand to the side of my face to help ease the sting.

"You win," I said. "What are you drinking?"

He paused a moment, but laughed. "You're a stubborn son of a bitch, but I like that. All right, let's do a couple Jacks."

"I think I need a straw," I said, rubbing my jaw where the pain from the slap was still radiating. "I can't feel my face yet."

Stroker laughed, and I chuckled as much as I could without moving my face.

We eventually became good friends because he trusted and respected me. I was one of the few guys who could walk up to him and say, "Let's go have a drink." The day I knew our friendship was locked in was when he finally walked up to me and said, "Hey Turk, let's go get a drink." That was as good as an "I love you" from him.

We had been drinking pretty heavily one night at the Backstreet Tavern when he opened up to me about the club. Stroker confessed he was about ready to retire from being the club's Sergeant at Arms. He was so tired of hearing all the complaints and found himself just telling everyone to shut the fuck up or turn in their patch. If they gave him a hard time, he would just put his boot up their ass and help them out the door. The only reason he had stuck with it so long was because Baby Huey wanted him to.

"I don't see Huey letting me step down unless I can find someone good enough to take my place."

"I don't know, Stroker. You're one of a kind. I don't know of anyone who could take your place."

He thought for a moment. "Well, Turk. How about you? You want the job? I can see you doing it."

I was astonished. "I don't know man," I said. "I've only been patched a little over eight months now. Do you really think Huey would go for making me an officer so soon?"

I know I had already developed a reputation in the club as someone you didn't fuck with. But at the same time, I stayed mostly on everyone's good side. I may have had an Irish temper, but I was fair and gave a man a way out if he wanted it.

"It doesn't matter how long you've been patched. What matters is if you can do the job. What do you think, Turk? Can you do the job?"

"I don't know, man. I know I can handle myself in almost any situation. What do you think, Stroker?"

"I wouldn't have asked you if I had doubts about you being able to handle it."

"To tell you the truth, Stroker. I would love to have your job. What do we have to do to get this done?"

"I'll tell Baby Huey what we want to do. Then he'll bring it up at the next meeting. Are you sure you're ready for this?"

"Is there something you're not telling me? "

"There's a lot of shit I'm not telling you." He chuckled darkly. "But the fact is, you need to deal with this shit as it falls into your lap in your own way. Can you handle this or not?"

"Fuck yeah, I can!" I whooped. "I'll call Huey myself and get the ball rolling."

Stroker gave me one of his rare smiles as we both did another shot.

"Cool, but let me call Huey—he should hear it from me," said Stroker, following the shot with a sip of cold beer. "Shit, man, I feel better already. I never realized what a burden I was carrying as the Sergeant at Arms. Come on, Turk, let's you and I get fucked up!"

"Shit, Stroker, I'm already fucked up!"

We talked into the early hours of the morning and learned a lot about each other. I guess you could say we sealed our friendship that night.

When Stroker informed Huey of what we wanted to happen, he was at first against it. Huey had a long talk with Stroker and tried to discourage him from stepping down, but Stroker finally convinced Huey that this was what was best for him and the club. Huey gave in and said it would come up for vote at the next meeting.

Then Baby Huey and I sat down together and discussed one-on-one what was going on.

"Turk, do you even have a clue about what your about to take on?"

"Pretty much. Stroker filled me in on what was expected of me last night at the bar." He still looked doubtful. "Look, Huey, I can do this."

"Stroker better not have talked you into this, did he?"

"No one makes me do anything I don't want to do," I said. "I've seen how Stroker handles things, and I can do his job and maybe even be better at it."

"That's what I wanted to hear, Turk," he said, slapping me on the shoulder. "All right then, I'll bring it up to the guys tonight, and we'll have a vote on it."

I was confident I'd get the vote. I knew most of the guys were tired of dealing with Stroker's bad attitude. I just hoped they didn't think I was going to be a pushover compared to Stroker. If any of them wanted to play that game, I would just have to prove how wrong they were.

But there had to be a downside to this, and I was beginning to think about how bad things could go when Huey brought me back to reality.

"Turk," Huey said. "You look worried, man. Relax. You'll do just fine. If I didn't think this was good for the club, I would have told Stroker and you to go fuck yourselves."

"Thanks, Huey," I said, my stomach untying itself a bit. "I guess that means I have your vote, huh?"

"Yeah, but I'll be watching you. Stroker kept these guys in line. Don't go and lose that or I'll kick your ass. You hear me, Turk?"

"It's all about respect, man," I said, holding up my hands defensively. "Nothing will change in that aspect, or I'll let you kick my ass."

Baby Huey patted me on the back as we walked through the back door into the kitchen. Out in the living room, the guys were coming in, one by one, for the Wednesday night ritual. Huey got Stroker's attention and motioned for him to come over. Stroker pushed through the crowd and made his way into the kitchen to where we stood.

"You two wait out back until the club can figure out what we are going to do about this shit," said Huey. He turned and pointed at Stroker. "I don't want you staring everyone down while they say what's on their minds."

"Can we steal some beers from the fridge while we wait?" asked Stroker.

He considered. "Keep it outside, and don't let the club catch you drinking during a meeting," he said hushed. "You know the rules."

Huey left us standing in the kitchen as he headed for the living room to get things started.

"What do you think, Turk? Should we get a head start on celebrating your promotion to Sergeant at Arms?"

I grabbed four beers from the fridge and handed two over to Stroker. "It's almost too good to be true. I've been patched with the club less than a year and already they're voting on making me one of its officers."

"Either you have what it takes or you don't. Hell, you stood up to me, and that's a first for this club," he said before downing the first beer. "You can have this shit. I'm actually glad it's almost over. I hated dealing with all the bullshit. I can't wait to be a nobody member and just ride."

I grabbed the church-key from Stroker and popped the cap off my beer. We walked out into the backyard for some privacy and waited.

"When this is all over, I owe you one, Turk."

"I was thinking it was the other way around, but if you insist."

We kicked back and finished our beers while we waited. We could hear a few members getting loud, but we couldn't make out what they were saying. Maybe it was for the best. It only took 45 minutes for the club to discuss and vote on it.

Doc stuck his head out the back door and yelled for us to get our asses inside. We stopped at the rear of the living room as Doc made his way up front, slapping a few guys upside the head that couldn't get out of his way fast enough.

"Well, the club has voted," Huey said, pausing for dramatic effect. "Stroker, you have more friends than I thought. A lot of the guys liked how you handled situations and thought you were perfect for the job." My stomach dropped sadly. "But...they respect your desire to step down. Turk, you got the vote. Turk is the new Sergeant at Arms. Get up here!"

I had expected to get the vote, but it felt even better than I had anticipated. I was overwhelmed at the thought of the club actually wanting me as their Sergeant at Arms. I couldn't stop smiling as everyone congratulated me. I walked through the crowd to where Baby Huey was standing, and everyone started chanting, "Speech, speech, speech!"

"All right, All right," I yelled. When the noise died down, I said, "You want a speech? Well, I have one thing to say. I know Baby Huey and Stroker have faith in me, and I also know that the guys who voted for me have faith in me, also. But if the guys who didn't vote for me think I have something to prove—well, you better think again. I don't have to prove shit to no one. I'll do the job the way I think is best for the club." I turned to step away, but then added, "Oh, and I have one more thing to say...Let's party!"

As time went by and the club became my family, I had all but forgotten about the reason I started this journey in the first place. My 1971 Harley XLCH Sportster that was stolen over two years ago had been pushed to the back of my mind. But I knew I had to somehow make peace with myself over the madness I felt in my soul for the person who stole my bike, but it didn't seem like that was likely to happen, so I let it simmer for the time being.

I was hanging out with Baby Huey and Doc at the local watering hole one evening when a babe walked in. Her long brown hair flowed down her back in a wave you just wanted to dive into. But she wasn't alone. Two dudes followed her in, but she didn't seem to be with either of them as she walked a few feet ahead and turned off in another direction while the men stood in the doorway.

The guys spotted Baron and yelled over to him. He seemed happy to see them. The cute little brunette was ignored as the three guys walked over to the bar talking and laughing. She hugged the bar alone. Eventually, she ordered her own drink, and that was my cue. I walked over just as the bartender sat her drink down.

"I got that, Vinny."

The bartender smiled knowingly at me before turning to the beautiful customer. "It seems you're drinking on Turk tonight," he said.

"You don't have to do that," she said softly. "I can buy my own drinks."

"Good," I said. "Then you can buy the next round."

She smiled, then looked over her shoulder at the two guys with Baron. They were too busy talking to Baron to notice me.

So she is with them. "Am I going to be a problem?" I asked.

"No, not for me," she answered matter-of-factly. "But they may not like it."

"That's too bad," I said. "Why don't you join me and my friends over at our table?"

"Sure, why not," she said, shrugging. "Did the bartender call you Turk?"

"Yeah, that's what my close friends call me. And your name is?"

"I'm Jen, nice meeting you."

As we walked away from the bar, one of her friends spotted us leaving.

"Hey Jen, where the fuck are you going?"

"What the fuck is it to you?" I yelled back.

The bar fell silent. The club members started standing up one by one, getting ready for anything. Jen's two friends looked at the force behind me and realized they'd be in deep shit if they wanted to pursue the matter further. The guy who'd yelled looked hard at Jen then turned to Baron.

"What the hell is going on, bro?"

"It looks like you have a problem with Turk," Baron said. "I suggest you take care of this little matter now." The dude wasn't getting shit from Baron.

The tough guy looked back over at Jen. "Are you with me or not?"

She considered a moment before smiling at me. "You know what? I'm so tired of your shit, Steve. I'm going with 'NOT.'"

"Fine then! Go fuck yourself bitch!"

I took Jen's arm and led her over to our table. The conversation was over as far as I was concerned. "Well, that went pretty smooth," I said. "Was that your boyfriend?"

"He was up until about two weeks ago. I broke up with him, but he begged me to come out with him tonight. I can see he hasn't changed a bit."

"Dudes don't change, babe. Love them for who they are or forget them."

"I think everyone knows that, Turk. It's just that sometimes you want to follow your heart, and it screws you up every time."

We sat down at the table, and Doc leaned over and gave her a long hard look. "Don't I know you?" he asked.

She looked confused. "I don't know. You don't look familiar."

Doc thought another moment and then, like a light bulb had flicked on, he snapped his fingers. "Yeah, you were Norman's ol' lady, weren't you? I met you a little over a year ago."

"How do you know Norm?" she asked.

"Dude tried to sell me some Harley parts, but I don't buy stolen shit," he said, leaning back satisfied. "I hate guys who steal Harleys. Those guys are pieces of shit in my book."

This got my attention. Just the mention of stolen Harley parts put a knot in my stomach.

"What did he try to sell you, Doc? Do you remember?"

"Yeah, it was a complete extended Sportster front end and some other shit. It was a while ago."

"Damn it, Doc. Try to remember, was there any sheet metal? A tank or a fender?" I asked excitedly. I was practically chomping at the bit.

"Oh, and there was a blue tank with Sportster written on both sides, but he had that half covered in the back of his truck."

"Motherfucker! That's my old tank!"

I couldn't believe my ears. I had almost given up finding out what had happened to my 1971 Harley XLCH when this just dropped into my lap.

"Turk, you never mentioned you had a bike stolen," Huey said.

"It's a long story, man," I said quickly before turning back to Doc. "Who is this Norman guy?"

Doc looked over at Jen.

"Maybe she's the one you should be asking that question."

I looked at Jen, and she looked like she had seen a ghost. "Look, I don't know anything about what he did or about any stolen bikes," she said. "I think I should leave now." She grabbed her drink and started to get up.

"Sit down!" I shouted. "Don't even think about leaving. I need some answers, and I want them now!"

"Don't talk to me like that!" Jen yelled back. "I didn't do anything wrong."

She was right. I had to calm down and try a different approach, or I wouldn't get anywhere. "I'm sorry. I didn't mean to yell at you—honest. I just got excited. Why don't we get out of here and go for a ride? What do you say? "

She laughed humorlessly. "Oh hell no! I'm not going anywhere with you. I'd end up buried out in the desert somewhere. I'm fine right here."

Baby Huey, Doc, and I broke out into laughter.

"Doc," Huey said, still laughing. "Let's leave these two alone before we get accused of being part of the Charlie Manson gang."

"Aw, come on, Huey!" Doc jokingly whined. "It's just starting to get interesting!"

A minute later, we had the table to ourselves. "I didn't invite you over for a drink to have it all come down to this. Can we start over?"

"I guess," Jen said apprehensively. "Depends on what you mean by starting over. Shit, we just met!"

"All right, fine. Let's not start over," I said. "Do you remember Norman talking to Doc about a blue Sportster? I know it had nothing to do with you."

"Maybe…I think it was about two years ago—maybe less. I'm not sure. All I remember is that he came home one night with this pretty blue motorcycle in the back of his van. I asked him whose bike it was, and he said he picked it up from a nobody."

"A nobody?" I barked a laugh. Who helped him?"

"Norm was with two other guys. I swear Turk, I didn't know he had stolen it."

"Do you remember anything about the bike?"

"No, not really," Jen said. "No, wait! Yes, it had a pitchfork on the rear finder, and it almost stabbed Norm as they were trying to unload the bike."

I couldn't believe what I was hearing. My sissy bar was in the shape of a pitchfork. That was all I needed to hear.

"Jen, baby. You just solved a two-year mystery! I love you!"

"Sorry I'm not as excited as you are, but I really need to go." She looked really uncomfortable, so I tried to calm down a bit.

"Look, Jen. I'm sorry, too. I've been going crazy for these last couple of years just thinking about who could have stolen my bike, and you have brought my sanity back. Please, let me buy you another drink."

She bit her lip uncertainly, but said, "I guess…But only if you stay calm."

"Sure, no problem," I said. "Just one more question. Where can I find this Norman guy?"

"I don't know. I think I've said enough as it is. Maybe you should go ask Red."

"Who's Red?"

She nodded toward the bar. "He's with Steve talking to your buddy. They're both friends of Norman."

I chuckled in disbelief. *This just keeps getting better*, I thought. "Don't leave, and please don't make me come looking for you," I said. "I owe you one, and I want to do something special for you."

She smiled. "I'll be here, but don't keep me waiting. I don't like sitting here alone."

"I won't be long, I promise."

I walked up to the bar and told the bartender to freshen up her drink. I then made my way over to Baron and interrupted his conversation with the two dudes.

"Baron," I started, clapping him on the shoulder. "Why don't you introduce me to your two friends here?"

"Why?" Baron asked, seeming genuinely confused. "You're not usually the friendly type, Turk. What's up?"

"I understand they know an old friend of mine." I looked them over. "You guys know my buddy, Norman, right?"

The one named Red shot a glance at Steve. He said cautiously, "Yeah, we know him. What's he to you?"

"Oh, we go way back," I answered. "In fact, he stole my bike, and I want payback!"

Silence fell but was broken when Red slammed his glass down on the bar. "Fuck you! I don't know what the fuck you're talking about."

Steve looked around the bar and spotted Jen. "Jen, we're leaving! Are you with us?"

She barked a humorless laugh. "Not a chance. I'm staying here!"

He snarled and started toward her. "You know what, bitch? You have a big mouth and I'm going to—UGH!"

I threw an open hand chop to his throat. I was tired of listening to his threats. He grabbed his neck and bent over, trying to breath. Red started running for the door, but Doc picked him up from behind and body slammed him to the floor.

"What's up with these two, Turk?" Doc asked as casually as if he'd just asked the time.

"They're motorcycle thieves. They're buddies with Norman, the guy who stole my bike almost two years ago."

"Stolen parts?!" Baron shouted in disbelief. "Is that what you two assholes came in here to try and sell me?" He kicked Red in the ribs and headed over for Steve. I jumped in between the two of them to stop Baron.

"Hold on, Baron," I said. "I need to know where I can find this Norman guy first."

I pulled out my buck knife and grabbed a handful of Steve's hair. I pulled him up and leaned him over the bar. The pain I felt the night I saw that my Harley was gone flooded through me and turned my vision red. I could easily see these two stooges helping Norman steal my bike. I yanked his head back and stuck the blade against the side of his neck. A red dot of blood formed at the tip of the blade.

I leaned close to his ear and said in a deadly soft tone, "I'm only going to ask you once. Where the hell do I find your buddy, Norman?"

He hesitated, and that pissed me off. With a little added pressure, the tip of the blade went a bit deeper, sending a trail of blood flowing down his neck to his shoulder. Steve winced and tried to pull away. I slammed his head down into the bar top with a loud thump. His knees gave out, but I yanked him back up before he fell.

"We can play this game all night," I said. "Are you up for it?"

"All right, man! All right!" Steve groaned, defeated. "It's no big secret. He hangs out at the Sunrise Cedars Bar."

I looked over at Doc and Baron and pushed Steve over to them. "Do what you want with the two thieves. I'm done here."

I watched as five of our guys dragged them out back. It didn't look good for them. I looked over at Jen, and she looked a little pale. I grabbed a fresh Jack and Coke and headed over to her.

I ran a hand through my hair and tried to sound chipper as I asked, "Are you ready for that special thing I want to do for you?"

She stared wide-eyed. "I don't know, Turk. You kind of scare me now."

I held out my hand anyways, and she took it. I pulled her to her feet. I wrapped my arms around her waist and tried to pull her in close, but she hesitated.

"You don't have to be afraid of me," I said softly in her ear, as she slowly fell into my arms. "Not tonight, not ever. That's not my style." I felt her body relax into my embrace as her head fell onto my shoulder. "You know Jen, I'm really glad I met you tonight."

"Why, because I gave you a lead on who stole your bike?"

"No," I laughed. "If you remember, I invited you to join me at our table long before I knew about Norman. You don't trust men, do you?"

"So, are you telling me that you're different from other men? Because that's such a line."

I smiled. "I'm a lot different from your average Joe," I said. "But that's up to you to decide."

"Well, I'll admit, you have a different way of handling things," Jen said, chuckling. "I hope I don't regret this, but can we leave?"

I smiled, and without saying a word, I led her out the front door to my bike. The ride back to my place was very relaxing as the cool desert air rushed past our bodies. It felt good to feel Jen's arms wrapped tightly around my waist.

When we got to my place, I had barely shut the door when she pulled me to the floor in her embrace. It was a race to see who could undress the other the quickest. It took us over 45 minutes to make it to the bedroom.

CHAPTER II

AUTORAMA

Jen had given me enough information to finally put an end to my nightmare. Not knowing who had stolen my Harley had been eating away at me for two years. Putting a name to this thief made him human. I needed to see his face and put an end to this pain in my gut. My mission was renewed, and I had direction now.

Steve and Red spent the night at Sunrise Hospital. They were told, in no uncertain terms, that if word got out to the cops or Norman about what we were doing, the next time they go to Sunrise Hospital, it would be on a slab.

Regardless of our warning, it seemed that the three of them disappeared. We checked the Sunrise Cedars Bar on a regular basis, but it always turned up empty. After a couple weeks, Baby Huey and Doc were on my ass to give it up. They figured if we took the heat off them, they might surface. I was pissed, but I had to agree.

It was irritating that I, once again, had to erase all thoughts of finding the asshole that stole my first Harley. But I had to maintain my sanity. I felt like I was so close to finding this son-of-a-bitch, and he just slipped right out of sight. I knew he was on the run, but I had my ears to the streets.

For the time being, though, I had other things to occupy my attention. The club was planning on entering a few of our bikes into the Las Vegas

Autorama Show at the Convention Center. Getting my 1968 Harley FLH ready for the show kept my mind somewhat busy.

My bike was completely chromed out with an eight-inch extended wide glide front end. I had installed an Invader five-spoke mag wheel in the rear and a 21-inch front wheel.

I firmly believe that I was the first one in Las Vegas to sport mag wheels on any street bike. The first time I saw the ad from Invader displaying their new five-spoke mags, I ordered the set right away for my 1972 Harley Sportster and now a rear mag for my Shovel. It took my bikes to a whole different level.

I loved to personalize my bike, and what I couldn't find in what little aftermarket we had back in the 70s I made for myself. Building your bike reflected who you were and your lifestyle and was limited only by your imagination. My Harley was always clean and polished. Even though most Harleys leaked oil from one place or another, my only leak was from the chain oiler. But, then again, my bike was a Shovelhead model and not an older panhead or knucklehead; those would come later in my life.

The Autorama Show was mostly custom cars and trucks—bikes were fairly new to the custom world. If you wanted a custom bike, you had to make the parts and build it yourself. Even the Harley shop only sold factory replacement parts, and the few custom shops that were out there didn't always have a custom part for your particular bike.

I had a badass Shovelhead, and I loved her. The show was on Friday, Saturday, and Sunday, which meant I wouldn't have a bike all weekend. It was the night before setup, so I thought I would take her out for one more nice ride.

After a couple hours in the saddle, I stopped at an old bar on the east side of town to wet my whistle. I backed my bike up to the curb and glanced over my shoulder at the bar's entrance. The sign above the door was cracked and the paint was peeling off, but I could still make out the name: Aces High Pub. I smiled and thought, "This has got to be my kind of place."

I pushed through the heavy wooden door, which announced my arrival with a loud creak from the hinges. I stepped inside and quickly took a mental inventory of the bar's patrons. Two dudes were at the pool table, and one was at the bar trying to make time with the female bartender. I relaxed my guard and found a stool two seats down from the lover boy.

The barmaid stepped over with a nice smile and wiped the counter top in front of me. "Hi, sweetie," she said with a smile. "What would you like?"

"I'll have a Jack and Coke. How are you doing tonight?"

"Oh, you know," she said, throwing a glance at the lovesick pup a few seats away, "same old shit, just different flies."

"I can see that," I laughed.

Cupid seemed to notice that the joke was on him, so he huffed and said, "What are you laughing at?"

"I suggest you mind your own business," I said, turning in my stool, facing him more directly.

"Yeah, whatever, man." He turned away from me and continued to drink his draft. The barmaid set my Jack down.

"What's your name?" I asked, turning back to the voluptuous bartender.

"Joy, and you are…?"

"I go by Turk. Nice meeting you." I took a sip—a perfect pour.

"Haven't seen you in here before. What brings you in here tonight? "

"Out for a late evening putt on my bike. Saw the place, so I thought I would stop in for a drink on my way back to the west side of town."

"Well, I'm glad you did."

At that, the dude two seats down started up again. "Hey, Joy!" he yelled. "Get back over here, so we can finish our conversation."

"Hold on a second," she yelled back in a less friendly tone than the one she'd been using with me. "I'm busy."

"Really? You don't look busy to me!"

"Didn't I tell you to mind your own fucking business?" I said irritated.

The change in his expression said it all as he slid off the bar stool and stepped over into my face. I sized him up as he walked over and concluded that he was no threat to me. I didn't even bother to stand up.

"I see you belong to one of those biker gangs. Where's all your buddies now?"

He grabbed a hold of my colors and pulled me into his face. He would have faired better if he had just walked up and punched me, but instead, he brought the club into it. Touching a club member's colors was a major insult and was dealt with accordingly.

Before he could pull his hand back, I grabbed and twisted it into a forward wrist lock. This dropped him immediately to his knees at my waist level, which allowed me to stand up and spin my knee into his forehead. His head jerked back and collided with the bar railing with a loud thud.

I looked over my shoulder and saw that the two guys who had been playing pool were headed my direction. I picked up the semiconscious asshole by his neck and hair and swung him towards his friends. He stumbled about six feet, then slid across the floor, face first.

"There's your buddy," I yelled. "Do we have a problem?"

"You're a dead man!" yelled one of the pool players.

They charged me. The one closest held a pool stick. I waited until he was ready to swing, then reached down for the bar stool and brought it up into his ribs. The immediate pain to his left side dropped him to one knee. I pulled the stool back to my chest and thrusted the legs into his face. He fell to the floor. Using the stool again as leverage with my arms, I folded my right leg and side-kicked the other jerk in his chest. The kick took his breath long enough for me to land a few good punches to his head to send him kissing the floor. I stood over the three of them and felt my adrenaline subside.

"You son of a bitch," yelled the dude who still had the stool stuck in his face. "You broke my nose!"

"Get up again, and I'll break you whole fucking face."

I looked over at Joy, and she was just standing there with her hands on her hips.

"How about another Jack and Coke before I leave?" I asked, regaining my seat.

Joy stood there a moment and stared at me, then shrugged her shoulders. "Why the hell not? You want a double?"

"Make it a triple with a splash of Coke. Are you joining me?"

"I don't think so. My boyfriend is going to raise hell with me when he snaps out of it."

I laughed. "No shit," I said. "One of those guys is your boyfriend?"

"Yeah, the last one you punched out," she said, looking over to check him out. "Do you make it a habit of beating people up?"

"Look, I just came in here to have a drink," I said, in my defense. "Actually, I get into a lot more fights than I want to. I seem to bring out the worst in people."

"Well, I guess it sucks to be you," she said jokingly.

I let the comment slide. After all, I had just knocked out her boyfriend.

"I still want that triple," I said.

When Joy handed it to me, I downed it in three good swallows and found my way to the door. Not until my Harley was idling between my legs did I look back through the open door.

Joy had picked her boyfriend up to his feet and was holding him back from running after me. I shook my head and twisted the throttle. My rear tire broke loose and sent gravel onto the porch as my Harley lunged forward onto the pavement.

I cruised up Boulder Highway to Charleston, then headed west for home. My mind drifted away from the fight and to the Autorama Show. I planned on meeting the guys at the Convention Center and setting up some kind of display for our bikes. I was excited for what was sure to be a fun weekend.

My bike was an everyday rider, so I rode it to the show instead of using a trailer like most custom-bike builders normally do. I actually didn't care about winning any trophies at the show—I just thought it'd be cool for our club to display our rides since we were so proud of them.

Baby Huey arrived early to sign us in, but before we could enter the building with our scoots, we had to disconnect the batteries and tape off the gas caps. We prepared the four Harleys and pushed them over to our designated area, taking a look around at all the nice displays people had set up for their custom vehicles.

We hadn't really planned on doing anything, but it soon became apparent that we had to come up with something. We couldn't just leave our bikes sitting there on the bare concrete floor.

There were only four of us—Baby Huey, Stroker, Hawk, and me. We had to come up with something fast. We went out back to see if something from the previous show had been thrown away. It was a shot in the dark, but what did we have to lose? Stroker hit the jackpot when he found a roll of used red carpet sitting in a dumpster. We cut out four pieces large enough to go under each of our bikes. Hawk got the idea to outline the carpet with the wood chips he found in the planters, and Stroker and I grabbed a few big rocks from around the flagpole outside to outline our club logo. Stroker had found some paint in one of the lockers out back and painted our club patch on the concrete floor.

"How are we going to remove that paint after the show?" Hawk asked.

"We're not," Stroker answered. "We're leaving our mark."

In less than two hours, our display was done, and we thought that it looked pretty damn good. We patted each other on the back and called Hiney to come pick us up. We were ready for refreshments from our neighborhood tavern.

The show was all weekend, and the club decided that someone had to be with the display at all times to keep an eye on our bikes. The doors opened at 10 in the morning and closed at 11 at night on Friday and Saturday. The show was open on Sunday from 10 am until 6 pm.

Everything went smoothly on Friday and Saturday nights. We were all enjoying ourselves as we sat back and watched the people walk by and check out our bikes. There were actually a lot of nice comments made about our scoots. We kept it calm—even with all the members present, we still wanted to keep a low profile.

We took turns sitting behind the bikes in the four chairs we liberated from one of the convention rooms. I enjoyed walking around, checking out all the custom cars and trucks on display. I especially loved the 1932 Chevy five-window coupe I saw sitting in the middle of some nice early rods. It reminded me of the '32 Chevy I had owned back in Virginia when I was in high school. I had been a damn fool to sell it, but I've sold a lot of shit I regret now.

Saturday night was award night, and we were all there for the presentations. I actually took second place in the custom bike division. The guy that took first place had a very nice ridged-framed Panhead, but mine was an everyday rider, and I was very happy to place in my first custom show.

Sunday came, and it was a lazy day for me. I had to get to the convention center for the break down, but I was in no hurry to get there. The phone started to ring, and I debated whether to even answer it, but I had to. Being the club's Sergeant at Arms came with a big responsibility.

I sighed and picked up the phone. "Yeah, what's up?"

"Turk!" Hiney yelled. "Where the fuck are you, man? The Mad Dogs showed up at the show, and it looks like there may be trouble!"

Any trace of laziness faded instantly. "I'm on my way!"

I got my shit together and had Gloria, the cocktail waitress from Cougar's Den, drive me over to the convention center. It was after 4 pm when we pulled up, and the place was due to close in less than two hours. I pushed my way through the crowd to where our display was set up. It was the last night of the show, and only a handful of our members had shown up. As I got closer, I could see a small group of guys gathered in front of our display.

I stopped to size up the situation. Hiney spotted me from where he was a few displays down and came over.

"Hey, Turk! Let's get over there."

"Hold on, Hiney. If shit happens, it might be best if we came in from the outside. Let's hang back here a minute."

He nodded. "Okay, good call."

"Do you know what they're all talking about?"

He frowned. "They're giving Huey a hard time. They're still pissed about the fight we had with them at Bonnie Springs. They told Huey that it's payback time. I believe they said they wanted our club banner."

I laughed humorlessly. "So that's what's going on, huh? Well, if they're going to do it, then let's get to it."

Just as the words were coming out of my mouth, the punches started flying. Three guys dived on Huey, and that was my cue. It was on.

All the guests in our area started screaming and running away from the scuffle. It didn't take long for the whole convention center to become aware of the fight.

As I was trying to reach Baby Huey, a Mad Dog stepped into my path and grabbed my vest. He cocked his right arm back, ready to swing, but I side-stepped to his left, blocking his punch with his own left hand. I grabbed a handful of his long, greasy hair and yanked him downwards while I slammed my heel into his left kneecap. He dropped to his knees, but I was hit hard from behind and fell on top of the asshole I still had a hold of.

The Mad Dogs outnumbered us, but we were hell bent on holding our own. I started choking the guy I was on top of while the guy on top of me did nothing but hold me down.

Eventually the guy with my hands around his throat choked out, "Get this fucking asshole off me!"

"Fuck you, bitch!" I yelled back.

Suddenly, the weight of the dude on top of me was gone, and I was free to stand up and punch my victim in the throat. As the Mad Dog went purple in the face and fell again to the floor, I whirled to see what had happened to the guy that had been on my back. To my surprise, Gloria had him by the hair and was swinging him around like a ragdoll. He was just beginning to regain his balance, so I kicked his support leg out from under him and added another kick to the face while he was on all fours.

"Thanks, Gloria!" I threw her a smile. "Now get back behind the bikes!"

I ran full force and tackled one of the dudes who was holding Huey, and we flew to the ground. While I threw punches into his face, I was taking a barrage of hits to my head from somewhere else.

Just when I started to think that we'd bitten off more than we could chew, a group of cops burst in, yelling with their nightsticks out. The Mad Dogs scattered, but we weren't going anywhere—our bikes were still a part of the display.

The cops yelled at us to get down on the floor, so Baby Huey, Stroker, Hiney, and I, still bleeding, did as we were told as they read us the riot act. Thankfully, one of the show organizers came up and defended us, explaining that we had caused no trouble for the entire event and that it had been the other club that came in and started the fight.

The cops were speechless as they looked us over.

I looked over to my left and saw a Mad Dog on the floor near me who had been unable to run.

"I'll see you in the streets, asshole," I whispered. "I'll be looking for you, so you best watch your back."

"Is that supposed to scare me?"

"It better, because it scares me to think about what I'm going to do to you when I see you again."

"Hey! Quiet over there," one of the cops shouted at us. "We're not done here yet!"

After a bit of questioning, the cops came to the conclusion that the Mad Dog Motorcycle Club had been to blame. When tempers simmered, I slowly pushed myself off the floor and walked over to one of the cops.

"Look, man. We just want to get our bikes and get our asses out of here. My head is killing me."

He smiled grudgingly and pointed at us with his nightstick. "Go on and get the hell out of here," he said. "I'm sure this won't be the last of it between your two gangs."

I smiled and shook my head, then turned and walked over to my bike. I put the cables back on my bike and took the tape off the gas caps. I walked over to Gloria and gave her a big hug and told her thanks again for helping me out with that Mad Dog.

"You gonna be all right riding home?" she asked.

"Sure, why wouldn't I be?" I asked. "You think this is the first time I've ridden with a couple knots on my head?"

"I'm not worried about your riding abilities, Turk," she said, punching my arm. "I'm worried those Mad Dog assholes might try to ambush you on the way home."

"Nah, Huey called the clubhouse. Reinforcements are on the way," I said. "We have a nice escort back to the clubhouse where an emergency meeting has been called. This shit will get fixed."

"Okay," she said as she leaned forward to kiss my cheek. "Will I see you later?"

"Of course, you will," I answered smiling. "I'll call you soon."

I turned and pushed my scoot out the roll-up door to the parking lot where my four bruised, but still-full-of-fight bros were waiting. We didn't have much to say about how we'd been caught with our pants down by about a dozen Mad Dogs—there'd be plenty said about that at the meeting, anyway. The cops didn't have anything to say either as they sat watching us prepare to leave.

The rumble could be heard a few miles away as our bros flew through town to get to us. As they pulled into the parking lot, I could see everyone was mad and ready to get pay back immediately.

"Doc," Huey yelled as they pulled up. "Lead us to the clubhouse. I need to follow you." Baby Huey's left eye was swollen shut and his other eye wasn't in much better shape. We all had our lumps, bruises, and cracked ribs, but our bros were finally by our side now, and that felt good.

Back at the clubhouse, we all sat around in the living room and talked about how much fun that fight had been. Win or lose, we loved to fight.

Hiney walked over to me, limping like an old man.

"What's wrong with you?" I asked.

He winced as he plopped down on the couch next to me. "I think I cracked more than just a couple ribs."

We all started laughing and poking at his ribs.

"Cool it, guys! It's not funny," he groaned.

"Hey Turk!" yelled Stroker. "What happened to your face? I thought you didn't like getting hit in the face?"

"What's wrong with my face? Did I get hit in the face?" I reached up and felt the beginnings of a couple goose eggs on my cheekbones.

"Yeah," Baby Huey chuckled. "I think in all of the excitement, I may have hit you a few times."

"Oh yeah?" I said, remembering the onslaught of blind punches I'd received earlier. "Well, that's the only way you'd get a shot in."

We continued to laugh and enjoy ourselves as all the other member arrived one by one. The club needed to know just what had went down and to decide how we were going to handle the situation.

Once everyone had arrived, all joking stopped. "Here's the deal," Huey said. "It's on with the Mad Dogs—big time!"

"Do you want us to take them out whenever we see them on the street?" Hiney asked.

"No," Huey answered, turning in Hiney's general direction. Both of his eyes were swollen, purple golf balls, and I doubted he could see anything anymore. "Let's not make this a one-on-one fight unless they initiate it. It's going to be a club deal for now."

"What's that mean?" Hiney asked.

"I want the prospects to go patronize their watering holes on the east side," Huey said, smiling devilishly. "But we'll sit back this next weekend because that's when they think we'll strike back. I want the prospects to find out where they are drinking and what they are talking about. I want to know everything because the next time we hit them, we're gonna cripple them."

"You got that right!" Stroker growled. "If they want to fuck up our bike show, then we're going to fuck up their lives."

After the ruckus of cheers died down, Huey said, "Get a hold of the prospects, and let's get the ball rolling."

Another chorus of whooping went up, and the party started.

1976

CHAPTER 12

FINDING NORMAN

I had been the club's Sergeant at Arms for over a year and was beginning to understand what Stroker meant about being the head of the complaint department. With every situation, my patience grew shorter. I soon realized that this position was turning me into what Stroker had become. I guess it was just one of the hazards of the job.

But on the other hand, I enjoyed the power this position offered. These guys would fight each other at the drop of a hat, and I was the one who decided if it was going to happen or not.

If anyone outside the club gave us a problem, I was the one who handled it, and the first name that came to mind in that department was Norman's. The way I saw it, he had escaped justice for stealing my bike long enough.

A lot had happened over the past year to keep my mind busy. Baby Huey had stepped down as club president, giving the job over to Doc, and we'd had a great summer riding to places like the Valley of Fire and Ash Springs. Not only that, but we even got to appear in Clint Eastwood's movie, The Gauntlet.

It had been a fun year, but I was more than ready to start my mission again to find that asshole Norman. I told Doc about the situation, and he finally said to do whatever I had to do to make things right, but he wanted me to keep the club out of it. My new mission to find Norman started that day.

Baron had been taken from us on a dark desert highway a few months ago, and he had been the only one who knew Norman's two friends, Steve and Red. I didn't have even a clue as to what Norman even looked like. At this point, my best bet was to find Norman's ex-girlfriend, Jen.

I searched the local hangouts, but she had disappeared also, so I decided to do what Baron had done. I put the word out at a few local shops that I was looking for a basket case or any Harley parts for sale at a good price. None of the bike shops seemed to know of any—or they at least didn't let on that they did—,but I kept at it.

Finally, after months of searching, my patience paid off. I was in a bike shop one afternoon, having a casual conversation with the salesman about finding a cheap Harley Electra-glide front end when my search came to an end.

The bell on the glass door rang, and we turned to see who it was. Three Mad Dogs walked in and made their way to the counter. I ruffled a bit, but kept my cool. Things had simmered between our clubs, and I didn't want to be the one to start the war back up again.

They started checking out the custom parts on the wall as I continued to talk to the salesman. I talked just loudly enough for them to catch wind of what our conversation was about. I knew they were staring at me from the expression on the salesman's face. He didn't like these guys or the situation, and it showed. I slowly turned around, leaned back against the counter, and looked them over. They were wearing their club patch, but I decided I'd play dumb and approach anyway.

"Hey guys! What's up?" I asked.

Narrowing his eyes at my dopey greeting, one of the Mad Dogs said, "Do I look like your friend, dude?"

I chuckled warmly, pretending to be unaware of the outright hostility the guy was radiating. "Sorry, man, I just wanted to ask you a question—"

"Why are you still talking to us, asshole?" the other Mad Dog interrupted me. He was doing his best to intimidate me, but I just ignored him and continued.

"I'm trying to put this Knuckle basket-case together, and I'm looking for some early Harley parts. You guys know any hook-ups?"

"Do we look like a parts shop to you?"

"Look," I said, "I've got cash for the right parts. What do you say? Can you help me out?"

"Either you're deaf or the stupidest motherfucker I know. Shut the fuck up!"

I smiled and stared the Mad Dog dead in the eyes. There was an uneasy stillness in the air as I waited patiently for him to make the first move. I glanced over at the other two and decided it was my move.

"Fine," I said with a shrug. "I'll find my parts somewhere else."

The urge to swing coursed through me, but I restrained myself. These guys might be able to help me find Norman, and I didn't want to blow that. I walked past them and out the door to my bike where I put on my fingerless gloves. I didn't have to wait long before the three Mad Dogs followed me outside.

"I thought you said you were looking for parts to build a bike," one Mad Dog said. "What's this?"

"This is my main ride, man," I answered. "I'm trying to put together an old Knucklehead basket-case that fell into my lap. Can you help me or not?"

"Don't I know you, man?" another Mad Dog asked as he stepped up to get a closer look. "You sure look fucking familiar."

Shit. "I've been in town a couple years," I answered coolly. "I've seen you guys around, so I'm sure you've seen me."

"My buddy here thinks you're a cop. You a cop?"

"Nah. I'm no cop, bud," I said. "My name's Rick. Are we going to do some business? Because if not, I'm going to be leaving."

One Mad Dog walked behind me on the other side of my scoot. The other one stood to my right, while the first one stayed in my face. I could feel my adrenaline pumping, and I relaxed my posture so I'd be able to react to a punch from any direction.

"You'll leave when we say you can leave. Now, what kind of parts are you interested in?"

"Like I said, man. I'm trying to piece together this pile of parts I already have, and I'm interested in anything Knuckle related."

They were quiet for a moment before the leader of the posse narrowed his eyes and said, "I might know a guy who could help you out, but it's going to cost you for the information."

"Do I look desperate?" I asked. "I'm not paying for information."

"You would if this guy had just about everything you needed. And if he doesn't have it, he can get it."

"Tell you what, I'll give you a finder's fee if I can just see what he's got."

But that was an outright lie. These assholes weren't getting shit from me for information. I could only hope and pray it was Norman they were talking about.

"I'll see if I can hook this up," said the first Mad Dog. "Meet me tomorrow night at this bar on West Charleston called Thaddeus Thud-Puckers. You know the place?"

"Yeah," I said. "I've been there a few times."

Thud-Puckers was a cool-ass bar that looked as if you would find it on a beach somewhere on the coast of California. It was wood-framed inside with all kinds of shit all over the walls. Everything from fishing nets, mining equipment, old signs and even a full-size canoe over the bar. Peanuts were free, and the shells were all over the floor. I liked it there because I wanted half the stuff they had on their walls in my garage on my walls.

"Good, meet us there at 9 and bring lots of money."

I clapped my hands together and rubbed them. "Let's just hope he has what I need."

"Don't worry about that. Just be there," the leader said as they walked off.

I fired up my scoot and tore off. I didn't want to get my hopes up, but I couldn't help it. Could it possibly be Norman they were talking about? I was excited to say the least. I went home and called Hiney.

"Hey Hiney," I said when he answered. "I think I may have found Norman."

"Who?"

"You remember. The guy who stole my first Harley."

"You've got to be shitting me," Hiney said, laughing. "Are you still chasing that guy?"

"Are you going to help me or not?" I asked, irritated.

"Sure bro," he said. "Of course I'll help you. What's the plan?"

"The Mad Dogs are setting up a meeting tomorrow night. I need a couple of members to back me up. No colors, though. I don't want them to know the club is there. Might ruin the deal."

"Who do you want me to get for this?"

"You call Grube, and I'll get Rotten Ralph. The four of us should be able to get the job done."

"I know I don't have to tell you, Turk, that you can't trust the Mad Dogs. They may just want to take your money."

"Well, the way I figure it, we're either hooking up with Norman or we're knocking out some Mad Dog teeth, so either way I'm walking away satisfied. It's that simple Hiney."

Hiney chuckled. "I always like your plans, Turk. They're simple and brutal."

"Remember, Hiney, no colors. The club can't be officially involved at all. Doc would skin me alive."

"Yeah, he would," Hiney agreed. "I'll tell Grube this is all on us."

"Cool, see you tomorrow night at the Whiskey River."

"We'll be there," he said, hanging up.

The following night, I cruised down Charleston to Valley View and pulled into the Whiskey River bar. My three brothers were already there, waiting for me.

"I want the three of you to head over to the bar now. Kick back with a couple of brews but don't flirt with the chicks or give the eye to anyone. Just keep the party at your table."

When I walk in, don't nod or even acknowledge me. Got that?"

"How will we know when things start to go wrong, Turk?" Grube asked.

"Trust me, I'll let you know," I said. "Now head on over there. I've got about 40 minutes to kill."

Grube and Rotten Ralph sped off, but Hiney held back for a minute. "So, what's the real plan, Turk?" he asked.

"Look man, I don't know what's going to happen really. Just be ready to back me up if I need you. If things run smoothly, just ignore me. I need to meet this Norman guy."

"Meet him? You mean beat him, don't you, Turk?" he asked with a large grin.

I laughed and slapped him on the shoulder. "That's putting it mildly, Hiney. Now get the hell out of here."

"All right then. Good luck, Turk."

Time started dragging after Hiney left. I thought about my old 1971 Sporty and how it had been a love-hate relationship. I liked my new scoot much more, to be honest. But she had been mine, and Norman had stolen her from me. That's not something I could ever forgive, just based on principle. I imagined him dismantling her to sell for chopper parts, and it made my blood boil. I wanted to meet this guy and get some good old-fashioned Sin City retribution.

After about 20 minutes, my patience ran out, and I climbed on my 1968 Harley Shovelhead. I had loved this FLH since the moment I first saw her. I sold my 1972 Harley XLH Sportster and bought this Shovel from Cecil.

I started my bike and sat there a moment, listening to her idle. It was like I had a second heartbeat. She was alive and talking to me, saying that she loved me too. I shifted down into first gear with a loud clunk and pulled out onto Charleston. I raced through my four-speed gearbox, just to hear the pipes sing. Six blocks later, I saw Grube on the side of the road. I pulled in behind him and shut my engine down.

"What's wrong with your sled, Grube?"

"Ah, I'm good, Turk. My fucking tail light fell off!"

Grube rode a 1956 rigid-framed Harley Panhead, and it'd vibrate so violently that shit shook loose and fell off constantly. I had to laugh. He spent as much time tightening shit up as he did riding.

"Where are the guys? Did they leave you?"

"Yeah, I told them to get their asses up to the bar. I don't need them around just to tighten a tail light. Go ahead and split Turk, I got this."

Since I was early, I knelt beside him and grabbed the tail light.

"Tighten her up for now, but when you get home, use longer bolts on the fender mount so you can add an extra nut to lock her down better."

"Good idea, man! I'll try that."

"Yeah—just make sure it clears your tire."

I watched Grube tighten up his tail light, and it brought back a memory of a time when Grube and I had gone camping up in Utah. On the way back, my bike quit running.

"Hey, man," I said, "do you remember that time my carb fell off on the way back from our fishing trip?"

"Yeah, I remember. Your manifold bracket broke, and you had to drive that damn bike all the way home from St. George, Utah to Vegas, holding the carb on with your right knee." He guffawed. "You can't do that with a Honda."

"That's for sure. I ended up with a huge bruise on the inside of my leg for a couple days after that," I said, laughing. "How's it coming, bud?"

"Finished! Let's get the hell out of here, Turk!" he said, standing up and brushing the dust off his hands.

"You go on ahead. I'll give you a minute or two head start. I don't want to pull in with anyone."

Grube nodded and took off while I sat on the side of the road staring at my Harley. Damn, she was pretty. After a few minutes, I swung my leg over her saddle and started her up. I took my time getting to the bar. When I arrived, I pulled around back and shut off the motor.

"Well, he made it," said a gruff voice that was coming up behind me. "And with a few minutes to spare."

I stepped off my bike on the opposite side I heard the voice coming from.

"Well, I see you three made it. Where are the parts?" I asked.

"Our guy's on his way. Let's just wait here for him. It's nicer out here, anyway."

I needed to get inside, but I knew that if I asked, they would get suspicious.

"Why don't one of you guys go in a grab a round of beers?" I said leaning casually against my scoot.

With a bark of a laugh, one of the Mad Dogs said, "Go get your own goddamn beer, dipshit."

"Geez, fine," I said. "Anybody else want one?"

"Sure, as long as you're buying."

"Three beers coming up," I said jovially.

I had to smile; that was way too easy. I stepped inside and headed straight for the bar, catching a glimpse of my bros over in the corner. I ordered four beers, and I held three of them up and pointed outside. When I saw them start to rise, I held my hand up for them to stay seated and put five fingers up for them to give me five minutes. The guys raised their beers and toasted each other. I knew they had gotten the message, so I went back outside and passed the beers around.

"What's keeping our man?" I asked, taking a deep sip.

"Just running late," said one of the Mad Dogs in a very unconcerned way. "That's just how the business is, man."

"Here's to you guys," I said, raising my beer. "Nice meeting you all!"

They didn't move to return my toast, so I just smiled and sipped my beer. "So, how long did you say you've been in Vegas?" one of them asked with a raised brow.

"Oh, a couple years now," I said. "Got discharged out at Nellis from the Air Force and decided to make Vegas my home." No reason to lie about that; it had nothing to do with the club.

"You ever ride with any clubs?" another asked.

And now I lie. "Never been asked to," I said shrugging nonchalantly. "Don't know about how to become a member. Is it hard?"

"Yeah, we just don't let anybody ride with us. There's a trial period you go through to see if we want you in. It's called prospecting. You want to prospect for the Mad Dogs?"

Ha! Holy shit! I thought. *Did he just ask me to prospect for the Mad Dogs?* I pretended to consider for a second. "Mmm, maybe," I replied. "Let's see if you can keep your word and produce some parts."

"Hey, asshole," one of them said. "We're not the ones being tested."

"Well, in a way, you are," I said. "Who is this guy we're waiting for, anyway?"

The leader obviously decided to ignore my insolence. "Dude's named Red. He wanted to prospect for us, but as you can see, he's unreliable."

Hell yes, I thought. *If Red is involved, Norman is probably only a step or two away.*

I knew Red would recognize me from the bad beating he got at the bar a few months back, but there was no backing out now, and I figured I'd just wing it if it came up.

And who knows? I thought, laughing internally. *He might be too embarrassed to mention it. I did bust him up pretty badly.*

As I raised my beer to my lips for a final gulp, the back door swung open and my bros walked out.

Shit. Guess my time is up.

One of the Mad Dogs looked up and shouted, "Hey! That's Hiney! He rides with the Noble—"

I hit him hard upside the head with my beer bottle. His legs buckled like they were made of gelatin as he collapsed onto the gravel. Hiney, Grube, and Rotten Ralph flew across the lot and practically tackled the other two Mad Dogs. With the four of us on the last two, they were taking a beating.

A moment later, headlights brightened the area as a car pulled up behind us. It was Red, and he was wide-eyed when he saw the ambush. He freaked out, threw the car into reverse, and spun out down the driveway beside the bar.

I looked back at my bros and saw that they had everything under control.

"Hiney!" I yelled. "I need to catch that asshole!"

"Go, go!" he yelled, still holding one of the Mad Dogs in a vicious headlock. "We've got this, Turk!"

I jumped onto my bike and threw loose gravel and dirt behind me as my rear tire screamed for traction on the asphalt. As luck would have it, traffic had him still sitting beside the bar, waiting for the passing cars to give him an opening. I pulled up beside the driver's window and pounded my fist on it so hard that I thought it'd shatter. Red panicked and floored it out into oncoming traffic, sending several cars swerving to avoid hitting him.

With the vehicles stopped all over the street, I easily pulled out and tore after him. I was right on his ass, and he was running scared. There was no way his car would be able to outrun my bike. He swerved in and out of traffic, but that was normal driving for a Harley.

The light was red ahead at the intersection of Charleston and Rainbow. He had no choice but to come to a stop behind several cars that were blocking him from running the light. I pulled up beside him, reached down into my boot, and produced my buck knife.

I banged the butt end against the window and shouted, "If you don't pull over into the next gas station, I'm going to slit your fucking throat! I need to ask you a few questions, so pull the fuck over!"

Looking like he'd already shit himself, he nodded obediently. I slid my knife back into my boot. I sat staring at him until the light turned green just to make sure that he'd really received the message. Red pulled slowly through the intersection to show me that her understood that the chase was over for him and made a right into a 7-11 parking lot.

I pulled in behind him and parked near the store entrance. I walked around to the passenger's side of Red's car and climbed in.

As I shut the door, I said, "Don't make me pull my blade out again because I'm done threatening you. Next time I pull it out, it will be to cut you. Am I making myself clear?"

"Yeah, very clear," answered Red with a slight tremble in his voice.

"It's not you I want," I said more gently, throwing some Good Cop into my routine. "But you know exactly who I want, don't you, Red? Now, I have one question for you, and don't stutter. Where is your buddy Norman?"

Red looked straight out over the steering wheel and lowered his head.

"He lives in North Town, man," Red said defeated. "Out by the community college."

"Does he know why you hooked up with the Mad Dog's tonight?"

"Yeah, to maybe sell some parts to a friend of the Mad Dogs."

"So, why didn't *he* come?"

"He wanted me to come out first and see what you wanted," Red said. "Norman likes the needle, man. He's kind of fucked up right now and didn't want to leave the house. If it was to be a big sale, he'd follow up with you later."

Tsk. Fucking slimeball. "Call him and tell him to meet you now. Tell him it's a big buy, and I want to meet him tonight. Also mention the fact that I have a lot of cash on me."

He turned to me. "You know he's going to kill me when he finds out I'm setting him up, right?"

"Look, asshole, *I'm* going to kill you if you don't make this happen!" I yelled, my patience wearing thin. "Besides, he'll be fighting for his life by the time I get finished with him."

Red opened his door, hesitated a moment, then got out of the car. I followed him up to the pay phone as he dug in his pockets for a quarter.

"Do you have a quarter, man? All I have is bills." He held out his hand showing me a couple wadded up bills. I grabbed the bills from his hand and put a quarter into his palm, smiling. He took the coin and shook his head as he deposited it in the slot and dialed the number.

Red explained the deal to Norman just like I had told him to do, but Norman still didn't want to come out tonight. He wanted to make the meeting for tomorrow evening. I told Red to tell Norman that that'd be fine, and we'll hook up tomorrow.

I needed to contact my bros at the bar, but I didn't know how.

Screw it, I thought. *I'll do it myself.*

I didn't like leaving my bike anywhere, but I was on a mission. I called the clubhouse and prayed someone would be there. To my relief, Baby Huey answered the phone.

"Hey Huey, it's Turk. Who's there with you?"

"Stroker and I are sitting here talking to Lance."

"Lance?!" I yelled, my attention momentarily diverted. "What the fuck is he doing there?"

"It seems he wants to come back in," said Huey. "He waited a year like we said, and he and his girl have come to an agreement about the club."

I sighed in exasperation. I didn't have time for this bullshit right now. My mind was buzzing. I was too close to catching Norman to lose him now, but I had a plan.

"So, what do you and Stroker think?" I asked. "You guys want him to prospect?"

"It's up to the club to decide. We don't care one way or the other. How about you, Turk? You want to give him a second chance?"

I thought for a moment. "I don't know, yet. Put him on the phone."

I didn't want to put the burden of a member watching my bike while I went to find Norman, but this gave me an idea.

"Hey, Turk," Lance said cheerfully. "What's up, man?"

"You want my vote to let you prospect?"

"Hell yeah, man!" Lance yelled. "I really want back in—honest, Turk! I've learned my lesson on loyalty to the club and—"

"All right, all right," I said, cutting him off. I didn't have patience for Lance before, but tonight I was especially short. "I need you to prove that loyalty right now."

"Sure man, anything."

"Meet me at the 7-11 on West Charleston and Anatolia, across from the Hush Puppy. No questions—just get here now."

"Cool! I'm on my way."

I knew it'd take him a little bit to get to us, so I looked at Red and pointed to the car. Red and I made ourselves comfortable listening to the radio. Alice Cooper was singing "I'm Eighteen," and it took me to another time for the moment.

The song ended and Red's nervous tapping on the steering wheel brought me back to reality.

"So, you're telling me that Norman is high on shit right now? Is that why he can't meet us?"

"Yeah, that's right, man."

I narrowed my eyes. "You like the needle too, don't you, Red?"

"Fuck no, man!" Red yelled. "I might smoke a little pot, but I don't stick no fucking needle in my arm."

"Does Norman keep a lot of drugs at his house?"

"No, he just buys a hit every now and then. But I really don't know how many times a week he does it."

"I don't care how much he does as long as he did it tonight."

"Yeah, man, I told you. He's fucked up right now."

"Good, that'll make things a lot easier. We're gonna go pay Norman a little visit." For a moment, Red looked like he was going to argue, but one look at my face stopped him; this plan wasn't up for debate. "But if you're lying to me and things don't go smoothly, it's gonna go very badly for you. You *do* remember the night at the Backstreet Tavern, don't you?"

"Yeah, I remember," Red said, wincing as he looked away from me.

Lance pulled into the parking lot and spotted my scoot, but when he didn't see me with it, his head went on a swivel. When he saw me in Red's car, he came up and leaned over to talk to me through the window.

"All right, Turk," Lance said excitedly, "what do you need me to do?"

"Just sit here with my bike. Don't let no one fuck with it," I said.

His face fell. "What? I drove all the way across town just to babysit your bike?"

"Look, I don't owe you any answers. If this is gonna be a problem, maybe you aren't cut out to prospect."

"No, it's cool, man. I got it covered. How long you think you're going to be?"

"Why are you still asking me questions, asshole?"

"Sorry, just curious. That's all."

"It's my fucking scoot! I'll be back!" With that, I looked at Red and slapped the dash. "Let's go!"

Red floored it and we veered out into the street. As we headed for North Town, my heart was beating through my chest. Soon, I would be face to face with the man who'd stolen my world.

When I saw the community college come up on our left, I knew we were close. We pulled into a neighborhood and went down the street a few houses. Then, suddenly, Red bounced across the curb, over the sidewalk, and into Norman's front yard. Then Red leaned on the horn. I grabbed his arm and twisted it back into a wristlock. He drew in his breath in a gasp of pain.

"What the fuck do you think you're doing?" I yelled.

"Ow, ow, fuck! It's our signal, man! It's cool! Let go!"

The front door opened and out stepped a tall, scrawny dude sporting a greasy ponytail.

My stomach dropped. "That Norman?"

"Yeah," Red said, rubbing his wrist, "and this is as far as I go."

Norman strode across the lawn and stopped in front of the car, staring at Red.

"Why the fuck are you here?" Norman snapped. "I told you we weren't meeting until tomorrow night, asshole!"

I stepped out of the car and got so close to Norman's face that I could smell the sour aroma of beer coming off his yellow teeth.

"Who the fuck are you?" Norman snarled.

My anger was surging inside me like a tidal wave, but I had to rein myself in and savor this. "You have no idea how long I've waited to look at your punk-ass face," I said through my gritted teeth.

Norman blinked his bloodshot eyes a few times, obviously struggling to focus on my face. "Really? And why the hell is that?"

Just then, the front door opened and we both turned to look. Out walked Jen. Spotting me, her eyes went wide, and she screamed, "Holy shit! Norm, he wants to kill you!"

Norman whirled around to face me with his dilated eyes as wide as dinner plates. I grabbed him by the ponytail and slammed his face down onto the hood of Red's car, leaving a sizable dent. I pulled his head back up and jerked it over into the beam of the headlights to get a good look at his face. He was now bleeding from his nose and teeth from the blow, but I was far from finished.

Red threw the car into reverse and backed out into the street, sending Norman and I tumbling onto the lawn. I had one good grip around his throat and another holding onto his hair as we lay on the ground. Norman was pushing against my arms, trying desperately to break free, but that wasn't going to happen.

Jen ran through the yard past us, screaming for Red to wait for her. He screeched to a halt just long enough for her to hop in before once again flooring it. They soon disappeared into the dark neighborhood.

I guess there really is no honor among thieves, I thought bitterly.

I yanked Norman to his feet and flung him across the yard towards the house. He landed spread eagle face down in the grass. He tried to stand up and make a run for the door, but I was quicker than his doped-up ass. I side-kicked him in the right kidney, which sent him head first into the front door. It bounced open and hit the inside wall with a loud crash. I stepped over his body where it again lay sprawled, picked him up in a choke hold, and dragged him toward the living room, pausing to kick the door shut behind us.

I looked around to make sure no one else was in the house with us but saw nothing but broken bottles and dirty needles. When I was satisfied we were alone, I tightened my hold on his neck and cut off his air supply. He started kicking and twisting, but to no avail. When I felt him getting weaker and starting to pass out, I let him drop with a thump to the floor where he lay clutching his throat, gasping for air.

"If you think I'm done, you better think again. You're not getting off that easy," I said bitterly to the pathetic creature at my feet.

Still, I let him crawl across the carpet and lean against the couch. He started to look around in a way I'm sure he thought was subtle for some type of weapon, but there was nothing in reach.

"Who the fuck are you?" Norman asked. "What the fuck do you want?"

I knelt in front of him and told him a story. I told him about how on a cold November night back in 1971 a blue Sportster was stolen from behind an apartment complex downtown—how I have waited for what seemed like a lifetime to find the man who stole my first Harley—how it had been eating away at me, day after day, year after year until that moment.

"Yeah, I remember that bike," Norman said as a smile slowly appeared on his face. "That bike belonged to some punk kid who was pretending to be a biker. I was in the bar with some friends and watched the kid leave, so we followed him home. You telling me that punk kid was you?" He laughed cruelly. "Man, you've aged!"

"I may have been a young punk to you back then, but let me make something clear to you right now," I said, his laughter turning my vision red. "The pain and suffering you put me through made me what I am today. Now it's time for you to reap the fruits of your labor."

His face fell as he grew silent and grave. "Let me give you some advice," he said. "Don't fuck with me! I have friends who will hunt you down and bury you. If you get the hell out of my house now, I might forget this little event ever happened."

I couldn't believe he was threatening me from his prone position on the floor. I reached for his shirt to drag him up off the floor, but he threw his arm up to stop me, so I just grabbed his arm instead. I twisted it into a reverse wristlock and forced him to his feet. I torqued his arm over, forcing him to lean forward, and I brought my knee up hard into his chest, sending his breath shooting out in a huff.

Norman found himself again gasping for air as he dropped to his knees. I dragged him by his wrist into the kitchen as he yelled at me between gasps for air.

"You're dead," he yelled. "You hear me? You're a dead man!"

I pulled him up by the ponytail.

"You know, your mouth is writing checks your body can't cash," I said emphatically. "You need to shut the fuck up!"

I let go of his hair and put both hands onto his already twisted wrist.

I leaned in, just inches from his greasy nose, and looked into his eyes. They were swollen and red, but he just smiled and whispered again, "You're a fucking dead man."

I felt the warm flow of blood rush through my body and into my head as I dropped my weight onto his bent wrist and heard it snap. He screamed so loud I thought the kitchen windows would explode.

"You won't be stealing any more Harley's with that hand," I said over his pathetic whimpering. "It's punks like you that make every Harley owner carry a lock and chain. You make me sick!"

"All right! All right! I get the message!" Norman cried! "What do you want from me?"

"Satisfaction!" I growled. "But I'm not feeling it quite yet."

Norman jerked away to get free from me, but I stopped his escape attempt with a sharp elbow to the jaw. I heard it break with a sickening crack as he went flying into the corner of the kitchen table. A large gash opened on the corner of his forehead as he tumbled to the floor.

Norman looked up at me like a pitiful old man and started weeping. He tried to talk, but his jaw wasn't working.

I grabbed his feet and dragged him out of the kitchen, leaving a trail of blood across the dirty white tiled floor. I pulled him through the laundry room and out the garage door. I stepped down the two concrete steps to the garage floor and pulled hard on his legs. His head kissed each step with a loud thud, one by one. I dragged him to the center of the garage area and dropped his legs beside his car.

His hair was matted with blood, and he was barely moving.

"Man, that's a nasty cut on your forehead," I said, clicking my tongue in a 'tsk'. "You should have that checked out."

I looked around the garage and spotted a baseball bat leaning against some boxes in in the corner. With a smile, I strolled over and grabbed it, tapping it against my open palm as I made my way back to stand over his mangled body. Norman looked up at me with tear-filled eyes as I raised the bat high over my shoulder and tightened my grip. He covered his head as best he could with his one good arm, cowering and shaking with fear as he rolled into a fetal position.

"Please, no...no..." he groaned as best as his jaw would allow.

What a coward, I thought. He wasn't worth it, so I relaxed my arms to my sides, letting go of the bat and watching it roll slowly away.

"Son of a bitch!" I yelled, sending my fist through the plaster of the garage wall. I was mad at the part of me that said that I shouldn't kill him; I couldn't fight that side. But still, I figured I could come back when this piece of shit was healed and start all over again. Beating him to an inch of his life on a regular basis seemed like it'd be a better lesson than a one-and-done gig anyways.

"I'm done with you, for now," I said. "But you better hope I never see your face again. You understand me? Stay the hell out of my world, or the next time I won't be so nice."

Noticing his car on the other side of the garage, I leaned over and patted down his pockets. Finding his keys, I pulled them out of his pocket. He made a pathetic attempt to stop me, but I just slapped his bloody hand away.

I smiled and tossed the keys up before snatching them out of the air.

"You stole my bike, asshole. Now I'm stealing your car. How does that settle in your stomach, dude?"

With one hand lying broken on his chest and the other hand holding his jaw in place, he slowly lifted his bloody head off the cold cement floor. He looked up at me and spit a glob of bloody spit at me in one last act of defiance. He grimaced from the pain in his jaw and gently settled his head back onto the cold cement floor.

"How's it feel watching someone take your shit, knowing there's nothing you can do about it? Bet it feels good, huh?"

After slapping the garage door button, I climbed into his Oldsmobile Cutlass and backed out of the driveway. Once I was out onto the street, I looked back into the garage and stared at his limp body where he still lay on the floor and considered driving over him for a moment. Before the temptation got the better of me, I pulled the shifter down into drive and floored it, tearing away.

I drove across town to the 7-11 and pulled up next to my bike. Lance jumped up from the curb and ran up to me like an excited puppy.

"Who's car, Turk? "

"Don't know. I think it's stolen."

"That's funny, Turk. Shit, man, you've got blood all over you," he said dumbly, his eyes going wide. "Are you okay?"

"Yeah," I said looking down at my red-stained clothes. "It's not my blood."

"Well, whoever's blood it is, I wouldn't want to be in their shoes. So what's the plan now, Turk?"

"I'm going home. You need to find Hiney, Grube, and Rotten Ralph. I left them at Thud-Puckers while they were beating the shit out of a couple Mad Dogs. Find them and call me at home. I need to know if they are all right and where they are right now. Am I clear on that?"

"Yeah, sure, Turk! I'm on it!"

I threw my leg over my scoot and sat for a moment, lost in thought.

When I snapped out of it, I turned to Lance, who was obviously waiting to be dismissed. "I'm going to take a long, hot shower and get some rest. Call me no matter what time it is. Go find those guys! Now!"

"I'll find them, I promise. I'll call you as soon as I do."

I pulled out of the parking lot and putted home at a smooth, steady pace. Damn, I felt good. *Damn, I'm going to sleep well tonight.*

I couldn't believe that I'd finally found the man who had stole my first Harley. It gave me some closure on this matter, but I knew I would be hunting him down again, soon. I was determined to make his life a living hell, just as mine had been the last three years.

CHAPTER 13

LATHROP WELLS

My hungry anticipation grew as my blade slowly sliced through the thin layer of skin, revealing the soft flesh beneath. I relaxed back onto the sofa and munched on the apple slice as Starsky and Hutch played merrily on the TV set. I was about a half an hour into my program when the thunder of a Harley engine vibrated its way through the walls of my house.

Who the hell is coming over to my place without calling first? I thought.

I reluctantly pulled myself off the couch and peeked through the curtains. My blood pressure immediately rose as I saw Lance climbing off his bike, leaving a woman sitting on the back.

I flung open the front door and glared. "Lance! Get your ass back on your bike and go find a pay phone. You need to call me before you come over."

"Aw, come on, Turk! If I do that, you'll just say no!"

"That's right. I'm busy."

"Hey, man, come on!" he begged. "Just give me a minute, will ya?"

Lance wanted back in the club, but the fact that he stayed with my scoot and found my bros the other night really wasn't enough to get my vote. He needed to earn our trust all over again. I didn't want it to be that easy for him.

Lance reached into his passenger's purse and pulled out a bottle of Jack Daniels. He held the bottle over his head for me to see and put his arm around his girl.

"I brought a piece offering. I want you to meet my girl!" he said. "Turk, this is Sharon. Sharon, this is the man I've been telling you about—Turk."

Slipping off the back of the scoot, she grinned. "Lance has been talking about you a lot over this past year. It's a pleasure to finally meet you, Turk."

I hated to admit it, but she was downright gorgeous. I couldn't help but wonder why she was with a guy like Lance. She walked up to my door and held her hand out. I took it in mine and gently squeezed, but she gave me a firm handshake back; I liked that in a woman. Without taking my eyes off her smiling face, I yelled over to Lance.

"You're lucky your girl is so beautiful. Now bring my bottle of Jack in, and let's hear what you have on your mind."

I hated giving in so easily but what the hell, a swig of Jack always sounded good.

Very few people knew where I lived and even fewer people were allowed inside. Lance was lucky I had a weakness for beautiful women. I knew he was desperate to get back into the club, so I decided to give him a chance at it, but I didn't want him to know that. Not yet anyway. The plan was to make him suffer a while longer.

Once inside, Sharon took the bottle from Lance.

"Let me pour you a drink, Turk. How do you like your Jack?" she said in a sultry voice.

"I like my whiskey on the rocks," I said, suddenly dazed by a moment of déjà vu until Lance broke my train of thought.

"What do you think of my girl, Turk?" he said, sitting on the couch as I leaned against the kitchen counter.

"What's that got to do with anything, Lance? Get to the point. What do you want?"

"All right, jeez! It's the club, man. I've talked to Doc and Baby Huey. They're willing to have me prospect again, but they said it only takes two votes to keep me out. They suggested I talk to you. What do you think, man?"

I gave Lance a dirty look and glanced over my shoulder at Sharon. I could hear her cracking ice from the ice tray for my drink. I looked back at Lance and leaned forward.

"Let me get this straight," I said. "You came here to talk club business with your chick. Are you fucking serious?"

"Well, I figured that since she was the reason you kicked me out of the club, I thought you should meet the reason face to face."

Just then, a hand appeared in front of me holding my whiskey on the rocks.

I could smell the aroma of the Jack as it floated amongst the ice cubes. I looked up at her and, without smiling, took the drink from her hand.

I watched her voluptuous hips sway back and forth as she walked over to sit beside Lance on the sofa. She placed her hand in his lap, and their fingers entwined. I could see why Lance was so desperate to save this relationship. She was a great looking woman, and I wouldn't mind having her shoes under my bed, that's for sure.

I took a large sip of Jack and felt the burn drift down my throat to my stomach. It was a familiar, comfortable feeling that I chased with a second sip. I set the drink down on the coffee table and stared at the two of them.

"Do you want a coaster for your drink?" she asked.

"No, thanks. I already have a water ring to mark my spot on the table."

They both smiled, and I had to smile back. I decided right then and there to get this shit over with.

Oh, what the hell, I thought. The club needed to decide his fate and I wanted to hear what everybody else had to say.

"All right," I said. Here's the deal, Sharon. If the members vote him back in as a prospect, the club owns him—not you. You're going to have to accept that. Do you understand?"

"Look, Turk. I want what Lance wants."

"Good, because it's going to be tough on both of you. Lance," I thrust my finger his direction, "you let me down on this, and I'm not going to be very happy."

"Oh my God!" Lance yelled. "Thanks, Turk! I love you, man!"

"Save that for your ol' lady." I rolled my eyes. "But you're not in the clear yet. The whole club still has to vote on it, and you know how hard it is to get the club to agree on anything."

We stood up and shook hands, then embraced with a hard slap on each other's backs.

"I'll do what I can for you, Lance, but I swear, if you let me down—"

"Don't worry, Turk. I won't! You taught me a valuable lesson about brotherhood and trust. I know what I want now. I need the club in my life." He turned his gaze to Sharon. "We both need the club in our lives."

"Yeah, yeah," I said. "Now get the hell out of here before I change my mind."

Lance embraced me again then stepped back, and his lady did the same. I held her a little longer than I had Lance. It was a different embrace, and she smelled a whole lot better. She stepped back and nodded, then without saying a word, followed Lance out to his bike.

I thought I might have second thoughts about having Lance prospect again, but I didn't; I actually felt good about it. Maybe he'd do great this time. When you have a woman backing you when times get tough, it makes all the difference in the world than to have to tackle the problems on your own.

The club was about family and staying tight. That's what held us together; it's what made the club as strong as it was. Prospecting was a period to see if you had the right attitude to belong to our family. It was a time we tested your trust, loyalty, and desire to become one of us. It's not easy to prospect, but anything worth having isn't easy.

The drawing for the Piece of Ass Raffle was getting close. I had made arrangements with Cecil to hold the drawing at his shop, Cecil's Custom Cycle Accessories. The tickets sold fast, and it was fun seeing the expression on the people's faces when we asked them to buy one.

Around noon on February 14, we all gathered at Cecil's for the big day. The drawing was at 1, and not a lot of people showed. In fact, out of the 500 tickets we sold, only 11 people showed up, and most of them were friends of the club.

I wasn't surprised and had to laugh when the winner was announced and he wasn't even present. The winner's phone number was on the ticket and a call was made to tell him the good news. He declined the grand prize of going to Lathrup Wells with the club and settled for the option of receiving $100 in cash instead.

We all booed him over the phone, then started laughing. He laughed and said he would have loved to go to the ranch with us, but he didn't think his wife would understand, especially with it being Valentine's Day.

"Valentine's Day? Is it fucking Valentine's Day?"

"Damn, Turk," Huey laughed. "You live in a cave, man?"

I had known that it was coming up, but I had other things on my mind besides some stupid sweetheart day.

"Well, I don't have a steady girl in my life, so I don't have to worry about that shit."

"That's sad, Turk," Hiney said. "You need to find a girlfriend."

"What? Are we in fucking grade school? Get the hell out of here."

"Just trying to help you out, man," Hiney said.

I punched him lightly on the arm. "I do all right, bro. Don't worry your little Valentine over it."

We were riding to Lathrop Wells with or without the winner. We thanked Cecil for his time and got ready to hit the road. As I walked outside with all the members, I saw Lance. Baby Huey saw me staring at Lance and got concerned for his wellbeing.

"Take it easy, Turk. It's cool. He's just hanging around to see if the members will accept him back."

"Yeah, I know. We already had a talk about that."

"Really? Well, he's not dead, so it must have gone okay."

"Have you seen his ol' lady, Huey?" I said, raising my brows emphatically.

"No, why?"

"Holy shit, she's a *babe*!"

"Is she what made you change your mind about him?" he laughed.

"Who said I had changed my mind, Huey? I just told him it was all right by me for him to hang around until the club votes."

"Hey man," Huey said, "that's cool of you. You know he's been staying in touch with me the whole time. He really wants back in."

"And that's all right by you? "

"As a matter of fact, Turk, yes, it is. He knows he made a mistake, but he doesn't regret it. I think the year he spent from the club was punishment enough."

"Yeah, well…we'll see."

I found Doc and asked for the winning envelope. Doc slapped it into my hand, and I went looking for Lance. I found him on his hands and knees cleaning Baby Huey's bike. I held the white envelope, which contained a $100 bill and the winning raffle ticket, up for him to see.

"Lance, do you know where Lathrop Wells is, out off North Highway 95?"

He stood up from behind Huey's Harley and smiled. "I sure do, Turk. Is that where we're going?"

"It's where *the club* is headed. You can meet us out there after you deliver this money to our raffle winner."

A flash of disappointment colored his face as he reached for the envelope. Then he looked up and smiled. "You got it, Turk. I'll take care of this and meet you guys out there. Thanks, man!"

He got on his scoot and roared down the alley.

"Hey, Huey?" I called over my shoulder. "How far do you think he'll get before he realizes he doesn't have an address?"

"I hope not too far. Does the stupidity scale measure in miles?"

We listened to his motor slowly slipping away when suddenly it went silent. When the noise started up again, it was coming in our direction. Seconds later, he reappeared around the corner.

The club started clapping as he pulled into the center of the crowd. He hung his head down as he walked up to me.

"Sorry, Turk. I got excited. I don't know where this guy lives."

"Well, neither do I, asshole."

"What? Then how him I going to give this money to him?" he asked incredulously.

"I don't know," I laughed. "Why don't you get his number off the raffle ticket and give him a call."

"Ahh, right!" he said, stuffing the envelope back in his vest pocket. He saluted us, then took off down the alley again.

I shook my head and hollered, "Hey Huey! You sure you want him back in?"

"Aw, come on, Turk! Give the guy a break!"

I laughed and straddled my bike.

"Let's get this show on the road. If it gets any later, we'll have to camp out at the whore house tonight."

The chorus of cheers and yells that greeted me implied that no one else would mind that too much. Hell, it even sounded good to me.

You wouldn't find Lathrop Wells on an ordinary map because it wasn't a town. It consisted of a bunch of trailers out in a field about 80 miles from Vegas with a very large grassy area out front for all the truckers to park their rigs.

Prostitution is legal outside of Clark County, and that's where all the brothels are located. It wasn't hard for the truckers to find them at night because they were easily recognizable by the red porch lights.

It was after two o'clock on a clear afternoon when we finally left Cecil's shop and rolled out of town, leaving Vegas in our wake. The air was cold and stung our cheeks as we hit highway speeds. The gang was in high spirits as we rode north for the land of ill repute.

Another nice thing about being outside of Clark County—besides the brothels—was that there were no speed limits out in the middle of the Nevada desert. When truckers came up on your ass, you had better move over and let them pass, or they'd ride your ass until you did.

My bike sounded good, and the road was just a blur under my feet as I cut through the cold desert air. Baby Huey and I were right behind Doc and Big Dave. I checked my mirrors regularly to make sure the pack was not leaving anyone behind. I watched as the guys behind me weaved in and out of their lanes to break the monotony of the steady speed. The rumbling sound of the v-twin engines around us vibrated through the air for miles.

Being out in the middle of nowhere allowed you to be yourself. There were no rules or restrictions to slow you down. This was the real sense of freedom. We were the only people for miles around, so we were free from all the eyes of judgment.

It was easy to get lost in time after a while. It's like being put into a trance from the sound of all the motors resonating together. All our Harleys melted together as one machine, carrying us down the highway on a wave of sound.

I was brought back to reality as Doc motioned for the pack to start slowing down for the left turn up ahead. I saw the ranch coming up as I shifted down to match the speed of the bikes in front of me. Dust filled the air as the bikes pulled of the highway onto the dirt parking area. A trucker's air horn blasted as though in warning to the other truckers inside that we had arrived.

I stepped off my scoot and stretched, shaking the cold from my bones. The first thing I noticed were the number of rigs parked in the ranch area. For some reason, truckers and bikers didn't get along. Bikers rode the highways to be free. I believe truckers felt the same way. It had to do with protecting the freedom of the road from others who wanted it also. I caught myself in a daydream and became aware of an excited bunch of guys around me. The truckers had better be ready for us.

Walking through the doors, I felt like a tourist entering the main attraction. I didn't want the guys to know, but it was my first time setting foot in a cathouse. I had ridden by a few times and saw the red lights on the porches, but I'd never had the need to inquire about the services, and I didn't plan to start now.

The bar wasn't large enough to accommodate our group, so we found ourselves three deep in the serving area. The guys were loud and pushing each other playfully, jostling to be served first. The two truckers at the bar looked pissed, but they wisely kept their mouths shut in the face of our 20-deep group of bikers.

After about 15 minutes, we were all putting down some cold beer, and the boys spread out throughout the lounge area. A couple of the girls ventured out to scrutinize the clientele, and the guys went into a frenzy.

I sat down next to Hiney and pointed to Rotten Ralph. "You watch, Hiney," I said. "I bet ol' Ralphie will be the first to go."

"Naw," he said. "My money's on Hawk. I know for a fact that he comes up here at least once or twice a month."

"Oh really? I took him for a lady's man."

"Oh, he enjoys working the herd in town, but he has a favorite up here."

I chuckled. "Sorry, but working girls aren't my type. You just don't know who they've been with—might wind up with someone who's been with Hawk."

Hiney almost spit his beer out, and we both laughed.

Baby Huey walked over with three shots of Jack. He gave us each one and held his shot up for a toast.

"I heard you finally found Norman the other night. Here's to sweet revenge!"

"Thanks, Huey!" We saluted our shots and downed them.

Hiney then held his beer up in the air and said, "Hey Huey! Don't forget about the three Mad Doge we fucked up that same night."

He considered for a moment. "Well, as long as the club doesn't get dragged into this, it should be all right. Here's to you, Grube, and Rotten Ralph."

Suddenly, Hiney jumped up and pointed to the girls. One of them had Hawk by the hand and was pulling him down the hallway.

"You owe me, Turk!" Hiney yelled, holding out his hand for payment as he plopped back into his seat. "I told you Hawk would be the first to go."

"Fine! What do I owe you?"

"Knowing you, I'd be lucky if I got away with just a slap upside my head."

"Oh, I can do better than that!" I said, putting him in a choke hold.

Hiney tried to stand up, but I pulled harder, and he fell over into my lap. The beers on the table crashed to the floor. Huey, laughing, jumped in, and the three of us went tumbling to the floor. Someone yelled "Pileup!" and it became a free for all. It didn't take long before we were all piled on the floor on top of each other in a wrestling match.

The two truckers at the bar had had enough.

"Why don't you guys grow up?"

He hadn't said it that loud, but for all the commotion, we somehow all still heard it. The horseplay was over as quickly as it had begun. Everyone stood up and stared at the truckers.

"Why? So we can be like you boring losers?" Grube said. "I don't think so, assholes!"

"I just meant that there is a time and a place for everything," the trucker said, backpedaling. "I don't want any trouble."

But the guys weren't going to let it end at that. We were always ready to fight at the drop of a hat, and this guy had just thrown a glove.

Grube walked over and leaned into the trucker's face. "What do you say, we leave it to the bartender to decide who leaves or stays?" Grube said, narrowing his eyes. He looked up at the beautiful young lady who was tending bar. He flashed a smile and said, "What do you think, bartender?"

She walked over and leaned into Grube's face.

"I'm not in the habit of running my business off," she whispered. "I think you guys should kiss and make up."

Grube leaned back with a huge smile on his face. "I like this one! Spunky! We need more beers!"

We laughed the would-be confrontation off as we took the beers from the bartender, raising a toast to the truckers.

"Hey, guys," Grube said as he raised his glass. "How about we learn to share the road."

The truckers looked at each other a moment, nodded, and raised their drinks to us. Everyone started yelling, and the party started again.

No sooner had we gotten back into the full swing of things than Lance came through the door.

"Man, that's a long ride alone!" he said. "I need a beer. What's up guys?"

"Hey, Lance, did we settle up with our lotto winner?"

"Yeah…kind of…in a way," he stuttered. "That asshole nearly got me arrested."

Lance looked like he was scared I was going to punch him in the nose, but I just laughed and said, "I've got to hear this. Get this man a beer!"

I put my arm over Lance's shoulder and pulled him over to the bar. Everyone gathered around to hear his story. It got quiet as Lance took a large gulp of his beer and wiped his mouth on the sleeve of his leather jacket.

"Well, after getting directions from the guy over the phone, I finally found his house. The street was lined with cars, so I pulled up onto his front lawn. I thought it would add to the presentation anyways."

"Yeah, no big deal. Go on!"

"Well, I guess it was a big deal to him because he came out screaming for me to get off his grass. And I have to tell you guys, I don't like people screaming at me."

"Did you give him the money?" I prodded.

"Hold on, I'm getting to that part!" he said, obviously relishing the attention. "So anyway, this guy comes out yelling at me to get off his lawn. I asked him what the big deal was, and he said that he worked hard to get it to look that good. I told him I was already on the grass, so it was too late to worry about it. So, he said to just give him the money and leave. But I reached into my vest pocket, and it wasn't there."

"It wasn't there?" I frowned. "What did you do with it?"

"I left it in the phone booth after I called him."

"You dumbass," Grube piped up. "Did you go back for it?"

"When I told him what I had done, he said to forget about it. He just wanted me off the front lawn. I said no problem and that I would be back in 15 minutes. I was about to pull out when his wife came outside."

"Was she good looking," I asked, grinning.

"Oh, *hell* yeah," he said. "I asked him if he wanted me to take his wife along to make sure I came back with the whorehouse money. She got all red and turned to him and said, 'What whorehouse money?' I told her that her husband had won a raffle at a whorehouse. I guess that really pissed her off for some reason."

Soon, everyone was in tears laughing as Lance told us how she started yelling at her husband for going to a whorehouse. The guy just kept trying to say that he hadn't been to a whorehouse and that it was just an optional prize of the raffle, but she wouldn't stop screaming long enough to hear him. The wife was yelling so loud that the neighbors were coming out to see what all the commotion was about. While she stood there screaming, Lance was sitting there, revving his engine to drown out her shrill voice.

"So I finally just shouted, 'Hey! Do you want the money or not?' But they didn't hear me."

Lance just kept revving the engine as the wife screamed even louder. He began inching his way in between the husband and the wife in an attempt to get a final answer.

"'I'm sorry,' I said, 'Did you want your share of the prostitute money or not?' but that only infuriated the wife even more."

She raised her voice into a hilarious falsetto and screeched, "'What kind of dealings do you have going on with bikers and hookers?' The more the poor guy tried to explain to his wife, the louder I revved my motor. I just couldn't help it—it was too fucking funny.

The husband finally got so frustrated that he charged at me," Lance said. "I gunned the motor and popped the clutch. The back tire flung grass and dirt from the guy's precious lawn into the air as I did a donut through the front yard. The husband was trying to stop me by holding onto my rear fender, but instead, I wound up pulling him through the neighbor's yard."

Lance said that his front tire hit a sprinkler head and threw the bike into a tree, pulling the husband down on top of the hot exhaust pipes.

"He started screaming bloody murder as he pushed himself up. That's when the engine finally died, and it got quiet. I looked up at the husband and asked if he was all right, but he just shoved me away.

As he limped back toward his house, both the neighbor and the wife screeched, 'I'm calling the cops!' at the same damn time, and I near pissed myself. I pushed my bike out onto the sidewalk and pumped the kicker three or four times, and she fired up. I banged her into first gear, jumped the curb into the street, and blasted out of the neighborhood laughing my ass off the whole way back to the phone booth."

"Well?" I asked, "Was the envelope still there?"

Lance reached into his vest pocket and pulled out the white envelope. "Anyone want a drink? I'm buying!"

CHAPTER 14

THE SET-UP

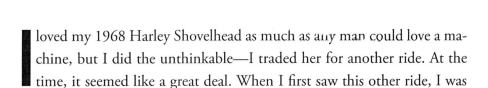

I loved my 1968 Harley Shovelhead as much as any man could love a machine, but I did the unthinkable—I traded her for another ride. At the time, it seemed like a great deal. When I first saw this other ride, I was blown off my feet. It was one of those "had to have" rides; it was a one of a kind Harley.

I was looking at a 1951 Harley Panhead in a trike frame—that's right, a three-wheeler. What caught my eye first was the 36-inch over springer front end. The neck had been radically raked to accept this extremely long front end. The engine was backed up by an original three-speed trike tranny with a reverse gear. It came with 16-inch dragster slicks on the rear, which was the finishing touch to this beast. The engine was tight, and no detail was overlooked when this baby was built.

The owner loved my scoot and couldn't wait to make the trade. I rode the trike around the block, and it was a done deal. The ride home was a memorable one. Everyone who was walking down the sidewalk—biker or not—stopped in their tracks when I pulled up. At every traffic light, every eye was on the trike and not the signals. I pulled into a gas station and threw her into reverse, backing up to the pump. It just blew people away.

I couldn't wait to get home and call some of the guys to brag about my new ride. Hiney was the first to show, and he couldn't believe it.

"So, you finally got yourself a Panhead."

"Yeah, I got tired of waiting for you on my Shovelhead, so I bought a Pan, so you'll have to wait for me now."

"Yeah, Turk, but this trike is so big, you'll have to ride at the back of the pack."

I looked over at my three-wheeler. He was right.

Shit! I'll be following everyone at the rear on all the runs. I never thought about that.

"Well, you know how I like riding at the rear watching all the scoots in front of me."

"Yeah, that's true. But hey, don't worry, Turk. I'll ride at the back with you."

"You know what, Hiney," I said, smiling. "I don't care what people say about you. I think you're all right. Let's grab a beer."

When we pulled out into the street, I realized more fully that my days of riding next to my bros were over. The only way we could ride side-by side-was if we took up two lanes as Hiney and I did tonight. No one seemed to mind though. No horns were honked to make us move aside. I guess they were smarter than I thought.

As we pulled into the parking lot of the Backstreet Tavern, my frustration flared again. The memories of riding my bike through those doors came rushing through my mind, and I knew those days were over with too.

We went inside and ordered our poison. Then, with our backs to the bar, we checked the place out. Since the Tavern was the club's main hangout, it was safe to walk in without checking it out before we came in. The bartender would be the first one to say something if there were to be a problem child in the place.

The jukebox was playing "The Pusher" by Steppenwolf, and the person responsible was standing in front of the box, dancing to it. I couldn't believe my eyes. It was Jen, and I hadn't seen her since the night she took off with Red while Norman and I were taking care of business. It was hard to be pissed at her as her fine body swayed to the music.

I downed my Jack and Coke and told Hiney to order me another. I pushed off the bar and walked up to the box, grabbing her by the shoulders.

"What the fuck are you doing here?" I asked, spinning her around.

"Well!" she gasped. "I was wondering when you were going to show up."

"Are you trying to tell me you've been hanging out, waiting for me?" I asked.

"Well, this *is* where I met you, ain't it? Don't tell me you've forgotten about that night already!"

"Oh, I haven't forgotten. In fact, I kind of missed you in a sick way."

I pulled her in close, and I could smell her perfume. My lips went to her neck without hesitation. She pulled away from my advance but smiled, undeterred.

"You *did* miss me!"

"Tell me something," I said. "Why are you here? Shouldn't you be with Norman?"

"Norman's pissed at Red for bringing you to the house, and he's mad at me for leaving him alone with you. You really busted him up that night. He spent almost three days in the hospital."

"Then I guess he's not happy with me either."

"Mmm, I wouldn't think so." She pretended to ponder. "But I haven't seen him since that night."

"Look, if you start lying to me again, you're really going to piss me off."

"Lie to you about what?" she asked, all playing suddenly laid aside.

"If you haven't seen Norman, how do you know he's mad at you and Red?"

"Red is the one who told me about Norm. Look, why would I lie to you," she added when I raised an eyebrow.

"So, what's the deal with Red?"

"He's freaking out. He thinks your whole club is after him, and he knows Norman wants him dead. He doesn't go anywhere unless he's packing."

I barked a bitter laugh. "Serves that little thief right. Norman got off easy, and it pisses me off that he only spent three days in the hospital. Maybe I should pay him another visit."

"Damn, Turk! He still hasn't fully recovered from what you did to him that night."

"Oh yeah? What did you hear? How bad was he?"

"Well, from what Red said, you broke his jaw and wrist and he had some cracked ribs. Oh, and he also had stitches on his head and a mild concussion. I think there were other things, but I don't remember."

"So, did Red say if Norman was out to get me?"

"What do you think, Turk?"

"I think I don't like the idea of looking over my shoulder all the time. I'm gonna pay Norman another visit. This is going to end now."

"Okay, calm down a minute, Turk. I need to know something."

"Yeah? What's that?"

"I need to know where *we* stand right now. Are we cool?"

My mind was buzzing about finding Norman again until I looked down into her eyes. Her eyes were the kind that could wrap around your thoughts and convince you to do bad things. And I was instantly captured. I wanted to hate her, but I just couldn't stop myself from pulling her in close. My body relaxed as we held each other.

"Yeah...we're cool," I whispered softly against her neck.

My lips went slowly across her cheek to her open mouth. When the kiss ended, I gently bit her lower lip. She was the therapy my mind needed at the moment. We were consumed with each other when the moment was ruined by a familiar voice behind me.

"Dammit, Turk!" Hiney yelled. "Am I going to lose you again tonight?"

We all started laughing, and I grabbed my Jack and Coke from his hand.

"Who knows, Hiney. Depends on how drunk I get. She just might get lucky." I said, winking at Jen.

She slapped my shoulder. "You asshole! You're the one who might get lucky."

I threw my arm over her shoulder and drew her in tightly.

"What do you say we both get lucky?"

Hiney rolled his eyes and went to find a table. For the next couple of hours, the three of us drank and had a great time. It would have been a perfect night if four dudes hadn't come walking in with trouble written all over their faces. They stood in the doorway for a moment, checking out the bar until they spotted us. Jen saw them staring at us and quickly stood up.

"I'm sorry, Turk," she said, turning to me with regret etched in every line of her face. "I'm so sorry."

She made her way over to the end of the bar as the four guys loomed nearby. It was a set up.

"You ready for this, Hiney?"

"Yeah, you lead the way, Turk!"

"Let's just get this over with!"

I stood up and met those assholes halfway with Hiney right beside me.

The first guy was the biggest, and he was mine. I let the big lug throw his best shot, but I ducked under it and came back quickly with a sharp elbow to the ribs. I grabbed the hair on the back of his head and executed a side-kick to the back of his knee. When his knees buckled, I pulled down hard on his hair, sending the back of his head crashing loudly into the edge of a table. He slumped to the concrete floor where he lay motionless.

A second guy didn't waste any time and tackled me from behind, sending us both crashing into the bar near Jen. She screamed as she ran to get away from the mayhem. The guy pulled me into a bear hug, but that's right where I wanted him. I leaned forward for a second, then threw my head back into his nose. He released me and started yelling obscenities through his blood soaked fingers.

"Here, this may help," I said, grabbing a beer bottle off the bar and smashing it into the side of his head.

He spun around as his legs gave out from beneath him. He fell forward to the floor, breaking his fall with his forehead.

At that point, everyone in the bar had either left or were backed up against the walls. I made a quick check for Hiney and found him on the floor, on top of another one of the dudes. The other asshole was standing over them both, kicking Hiney in the head. He looked up just in time to see me coming at him. A look of shock came over his face when he realized that his two other buddies were no longer in the game.

He made his way towards me, his look of surprise fading into onc of anger. We charged at each other like raging bulls and our bodies collided, sending tables and chairs flying. I slipped his first two punches, but he caught me with the third one. I staggered back a step and tasted blood in my mouth. I smiled and spit a wad of blood on his boot.

In a fit of rage, he came at me swinging with everything he had. I dodged his attack and tackled him at the waist. I picked him all the way up and threw him backwards over my shoulder. He landed head first onto the hard floor, sending him into a daze. It lasted long enough for me to boot him in the jaw for Hiney.

I turned to check on my bro and saw him standing over the last guy with a pool stick in his hand.

"Hey, Hiney, you okay? "

"Yeah, Turk. This one had a hard head," he said, tossing the pool cue aside.

"Well, Hiney. You can't beat an old fashion pool stick to soften a hard head."

Hiney and I gave each other a well-deserved hug and slap on the back.

"Yo Turk!" the bartender yelled. "I'm calling the cops! You two need to split. These dudes gotta pay for the damages."

"Yeah, go ahead. We're out of here!"

I looked around the bar for Jen, but she was gone. She had some explaining to do, and I wanted answers. I told Hiney to check out front but to get the hell out of here if he didn't see her. I ran for the back door and kicked it open. Once in the alley, I saw her over in the railroad yard, running across the tracks. I gave chase.

I hopped the fence and made my way to the tracks. She turned, saw me coming and screamed. She started crying, which made running almost impossible for her. She ran as fast as she could, but I was catching up.

She turned one more time and saw that I was right behind her. She stopped running and turned to face me. Jen had her hands extended out in front of her to try and keep me at a distance.

"Oh my God, Turk!" she wailed. "Please don't hurt me! I didn't want to do it but Norman made me. You gotta believe me! Turk, please!"

She fell to her knees, crying out of control, but that didn't soften me up. I grabbed her arms and pulled her to her feet.

"How did he *make* you set me up? How could you just sit there with me tonight, knowing that people were coming to kick my ass? What the hell is wrong with you?"

I shook her as I questioned her but caught myself and stopped. She was hysterical and couldn't speak.

"Look, I'm not going to hurt you," I said in as calm a voice as I could muster. "That's not what I do—you know that. Just calm down."

It took a few minutes and a lot more persuading, but she finally brought it down to just a whimper. "Turk, I really didn't want to do it. I don't know how to explain it. I swear. Please believe me!"

"The truth is I don't need to believe you because I don't give a fuck about you."

"Come on, Turk. Now you're lying! I made a mistake but only to save my ass. I didn't know what else to do."

"That's because you have no loyalty. You fall apart when you have to put friendship on the line. Life is about having honor and dignity and sometimes that requires sacrifices. And you have none of these qualities. I'm so done with you. I could never trust you."

I let go of her arms and watched her collapse onto the tracks. She started crying again as her head drooped.

"What do I do now, Turk?" she yelled through her tears.

I turned and started to walk away. I looked over my shoulder and yelled back at her, "Go back to Norman. He's all you have now."

"You bastard!" she screamed. "Fuck you!"

I kept walking and didn't look back.

At the next club meeting a couple days later, I filled the bros in on what had happened to Hiney and me. Doc was pissed to say the least. He had already heard about it from an unlikely source.

"I told you to take care of your problem on your own, Turk!" he yelled. "But instead, you drag the club into it and start another war with the Mad Dogs. You fucked up, man!"

"How the fuck do you figure I started another war with the Mad Dogs?"

"A Mad Dog prospect was sent to me with the info. You and a couple other members—whose names I won't mention—jumped three Mad Dogs at Thud-Puckers last week and beat their asses. Then, a couple nights ago, Hiney and you got into a beef with a couple more and stomped their asses."

"Woah, wait a minute, Doc!" I said. "That's not how it happened."

"I don't care about the details. Baby Huey told me you were a loose cannon and that I should watch you. Now I believe him!"

I looked over at Huey, and he just shrugged his shoulders.

"Are you guys really turning on me just because a couple Mad Dogs got their asses beat?"

"Turk!" Doc yelled. "You're missing the point! We've been riding for about a year now with an unwritten truce with the Mad Dogs. I don't know about you, but I enjoy riding around without looking over my shoulder. But that's over now thanks to you."

"I don't know what to tell you, Doc. You told me to do what it took to get my head straight, and now you're crying about it."

"I'm sick and tired of your insults. In fact, the whole club is tired of your holier-than-thou attitude. I've had more complaints about you than any other member."

"I guess that means I'm doing my job!"

I looked around at everyone and shook my head in disgust.

"Who here has a problem with me?" I shouted to the room.

"Back off, Turk!" Doc growled. "I've decided to have the club take a vote to decide if you leave or stay. Get your ass up here beside me."

I was speechless. *Holy shit…really?*

I walked through the crowd to the front of the living room.

"Listen up, everyone," Doc said. "Here's the deal. If Turk walks from this, we're at war with the Mad Dogs. They don't scare me, but like I said, I enjoyed the peace. We need to discuss what needs to be done to put this issue to rest and what's best for the whole club and not just Turk."

As my shock faded, I calmed down and thought about what I had done. Now that I looked back on it, I guess I was kind of on a rampage. But that's how we did things when Baby Huey was Prez. Doc seemed more politically inclined, and I didn't like it.

"All right guys," I said. "This may take some time, so I'll leave you to your voting. I'll be at the bar, so let me know what you decide."

"Do you want to say something on your behave before we vote?" Doc asked.

"It's simple," I said. "Someone stole my Harley. I found him and beat his ass. He just happened to be good friends with the Mad Dogs, but I didn't give a shit—he was going to pay. He had four Mad Dog's jump Hiney and me, so we took them out.

"That's it in a nutshell." I shrugged. "Think what you want, but if it happened to you, I bet you would do the same thing. If you guys want to vote me out, then fine. But I don't ever remember making a deal to keep the Mad Dogs happy. I'll be at the bar waiting for your decision."

As I walked out of the clubhouse, all I could think about was how good that shot of Jack was going to taste. I climbed aboard that damn three-wheeler of mine and headed for the Backstreet Tavern. I had owned this trike for less than a week and was already sick of it.

I sat alone in the bar with nothing but a rock glass full of Jack Daniels keeping me company. The bartender realized that I needed some space, so he kept the other customers entertained. I knew I was going to be voted out of the club, so I was mentally trying to prepare myself for it.

I didn't associate with every member in the club, but I had many good friends like Hiney, Grube, and Rotten Ralph. I knew that they would always be my friends, regardless of the outcome of the vote. I looked back at my life over the years with the club, and it had been quite a ride. I worked hard to get where I was.

You know what? I'll be damned if I'm going to take this lying down.

I picked up my money and slid the bartender a couple more bucks. I grabbed my rock glass and downed the rest of my Jack before heading for the door. I was halfway there when Hiney came walking in.

I stopped in my tracks. "Well, what's the verdict?" I asked, my heart hammering in my chest.

He shook his head. "Doc said for me to keep my mouth shut and bring you back."

"Fine," I said. "Let's ride."

I was buzzed and mentally tired, so my give-a-shit-factor went out the window. I didn't want to give up my patch, and I was afraid of what I might do if they asked me for it.

I walked into the clubhouse and went straight to the front to stand next to Doc.

"Turk, what is it about you that most of these guys love? I just don't get it."

"What's that mean, Doc?"

"What I'm trying to say is that I guess we're at war with the Mad Dogs."

"Look, I want what's best for the club. If you guys want me out, I'm gone. I don't want the club to go to war with the Mad Dogs just because of me."

Doc barked a laugh. "It's a bit too late for that. Besides, the club has already voted, and you're not going anywhere.

Thank. God.

I felt like a huge weight had been lifted from my shoulders. I began to realize just how much this club meant to me. You can never take anything in life for granted. It can disappear from your life at any moment.

"We love ya, Turk," a voice from the back of the room shouted, and everyone joined in with clapping and whistling. I put my hand up for them to stop and bowed to them in a noble gesture.

"Okay, Doc," I said clapping my hands and rubbing them together. "What's the plan with the Mad Dogs? Do we start kicking their asses?"

"Turk, that's such a typical Sergeant at Arm solution. No, we set up a meeting with them. We try to get to the bottom of this, and if they don't like it, *then* it's on."

"I've still got unfinished business with Norman."

"Damn it Turk!" Doc yelled. "No, you don't! As the club Prez, I'm ordering you to stay away from him. Is that clear?"

"Yeah, yeah," I grumbled. "But if he comes after me, that's a different story, right?"

"If he comes after you, *I'll* kill him. How's that, Turk?" he said.

"That's just what I wanted to hear," I said, smiling. "Now, I want to go to this meeting with you guys."

"I think it would be a good idea. You, Baby Huey, Stroker, and I will settle this once and for all with the Mad Dogs."

We set up the meeting for that weekend at the Railroad Pass Casino, a small spot halfway between Las Vegas and Boulder City. Since it was out in the middle of nowhere, it was a good distance from the cops. If anything went sour, this would be the best place for it to happen. And that's how we liked it.

We didn't trust the Mad Dogs—or anyone outside the club for that matter—so we had a couple of prospects arrive early. They were told to dress like citizens and play the slots nearby, just in case we needed back up.

When the night arrived, we found ourselves in the bar having a few drinks at a table across from a couple of Mad Dogs. They were trying hard to make a name for themselves in Vegas, and because of that, the cops had become more interested in them than us. I guess they figured that was the price they had to pay for a city's respect and fear.

The first name out of the Mad Dog Prez's mouth was mine.

"This guy, Turk, is he one of your guys here tonight?" Snake asked.

I didn't like how my name sounded in his mouth, so I snapped, "Yeah, I'm sitting right here, you motherf—"

"Turk! Let me handle this," Doc cut in. Turning his full attention to Snake, he said, "If you have a beef with Turk, you have a beef with all of us."

"Oh, I remember you," Snake said, his eyes narrowing at me. "You were the asshole who pretended to be a bartender a couple years back at the Backstreet Tavern. You were just a prospect back then."

"Yeah," I said. "I've come a long way since then."

"Well, it seems you're the reason we are here tonight," he said before looking back at Doc. "It seems you can't control your members."

"Well, it seems to me that you can't either," Doc responded. "We both know what happened at the Tavern the other night. Your boys went there to ambush Turk, didn't they?"

"And your boys started it by jumping our guys at Thud-Puckers," Snake growled.

"Look," I said, jumping in before tempers flared too hot. "We can go back and forth blaming each other for this and that, but what it all boils down to is Norman."

"Norman?" Snake seemed genuinely confused. "Who the fuck is Norman?"

"He's your club's thieving parts man," I said. "Your boys at Thud-Puckers were trying to sell me stolen parts, and I didn't like it.

"I didn't have a beef with them; I just wanted Norman. But the shit hit the fan. In any case, it had nothing to do with the club. Norman sent your boys after me at the Backstreet. I didn't know your guys were working for Norman."

"The fuck they do!" Snake yelled. "We don't answer to no one, asshole."

"Then my business is with Norman and not the Mad Dogs," I said, shrugging.

"I think your business is done, Turk," Doc said. "This needs to end here and now. Are we on the same page or not, Snake?"

"To tell you the truth, Doc, we would love to have this end here and now. But how do I know I can trust you?"

Doc turned to me. "Turk, are you done with this bullshit now?"

"Yeah, I'm done with the Mad Dog bullshit…but I still want Norman. Do you have a problem with that, Snake?"

"What is it about 'it's over' that you don't understand, Turk!?" Doc yelled.

Snake just smiled and threw back his shot of Tequila Gold.

"He's your boy, Doc," Snake said. "Can you handle him?"

"Let me worry about Turk," Doc said. "Are we good?"

"Yeah, we're good for now," Snake said standing up. "Let's go boys!"

The Mad Dogs left the bar and headed out the door. Doc motioned for the prospects to follow them out and help the other prospects keep an eye on our bikes.

"All right, listen up, Turk," Doc said gravely. "If Norman comes after you, the whole club will back you. If you go after him, you may lose your patch. Am I clear?"

"Yeah, I'm good with that, Doc. It's over."

I really didn't like this, but it was bigger than me. It was for the good of the club, and that was good enough for me for now.

We all walked outside, and the night air felt good. I kicked my Panhead Trike to life and sat there as the others started up their two-wheel sleds. Damn, I hated this three-wheeler.

CHAPTER 15

LEAVING

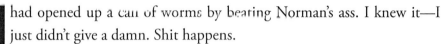

I had opened up a can of worms by beating Norman's ass. I knew it—I just didn't give a damn. Shit happens.

I wasn't sure how I would react if I ran into Norman again, but I would deal with that when the time came. At the moment, my mission was over, and I could get on with my life. The only thing I had to do now was sell my pain-in-the-ass three-wheeler.

I had owned it for a few months, and it was still a hit out on the road with everybody. I got plenty of compliments and questions about how it ran every time I took her out. I really didn't think I would have too much of a problem selling her.

I was actually embarrassed that I traded my scoot for it, but I had to get the word out that I wanted to sell it without people knowing that I felt like I'd made a big mistake. I was preparing to put my trike up for sell through the club and take the jokes from the guys for selling so fast when Hiney saved my ass.

We were sitting at the Tavern having a few drinks, and I was explaining to him how I wanted to dump the trike when he asked me if I had talked to Lil' Mike about wanting to sell my trike. I told him that I had just recently decided to sell it. Apparently, Lil' Mike had said on several occasions that he would love to own my trike. And to top it off, Lil' Mike owned a 1968 Harley FLH. I couldn't believe my ears.

"Hiney, you think he would trade his Shovel for my trike?"

"I'll give him a call now," Hiney said. "But are you sure? I thought you loved that trike."

"I just miss my ol' 1968 Shovelhead, and if Lil' Mike wants to trade his '68 for the trike, I'm coming around full circle."

I ordered a double Jack and Coke while Hiney tried to get a hold of Lil' Mike. I still couldn't get over the fact that another '68 Harley was going to drop into my lap. I tried hard to picture what it looked like, but it was just a blur in my mind.

Hiney came back to the table, sat down, and took a long swig from his beer. When he finished, he slowly set the bottle down and wiped his mouth with his sleeve. Then he just sat there staring at me without saying a word.

He was torturing me for fun. "What the fuck, man?" I yelled. "What did he say?"

"Oh, I'm sorry. I forgot what we were talking about."

"You think this is funny? Come on, man! You're killing me! What's he going to do?"

Hiney laughed. "Calm down, Turk! He's on his way over. He wants to work out a deal with you."

I whooped and slapped the table. This was too good to be true. Again, I searched my mind to remember what Lil' Mike's scoot looked like, but it didn't click. But I really didn't care what it looked like, I was going to fix it the way I wanted it anyway.

"Let's go outside and wait for him," I said. "I'm too antsy to just sit here."

We walked outside, and I looked over at my ride.

The trike looked really good, even just sitting there in all her glory. The huge front end was a masterpiece and was a great selling point. I needed to calm myself down and make sure I didn't jump into another mistake.

Twenty minutes later, Lil' Mike pulled up.

"It's good to finally get to talk to you about the trike, Turk," Lil' Mike said. "You're not an easy man to approach a lot of the time."

I chuckled. "Yeah, it comes with the job. How's the bike running? Why do you want to trade it for my trike?" I didn't want to sound too anxious, but I couldn't stop staring at his bike to see what kind of shape it was in.

"My bike runs great—honest, Turk. It doesn't have a lot of chrome, but she's a runner." He walked over to get a better look at my trike. "This is the coolest trike I have ever seen. I love the front end."

I couldn't wait any longer. "So, do you want to trade straight across? Bike for bike?" I asked.

"Well, I don't have any extra cash, so I was hoping my bike would be enough for a trade straight across."

Is this really happening, I thought. *This can't be real.*

I looked his bike over, and it was almost a twin to my old '68 FLH. It had a different paint job and handlebars, but that would be an easy fix. I wanted to do the deal now, but I had to look a little apprehensive.

"I don't know, man," I said, rubbing my chin pensively. "I just decided to sell her tonight. Maybe I should wait and see what other offers I might be able to get."

"Aw, come on, Turk! What will it take to swing his deal tonight?" Lil' Mike asked.

"I don't know. Maybe if you had the title in your hand, it could happen tonight."

He reached right into his wallet and brought out the title. He eagerly held it out for me to see.

"You need to sign it," I said.

He was smiling from ear to ear. "I'll be right back!" He ran into the bar for a pen.

I looked at Hiney and smiled.

"You just *had* to make him sweat a little, didn't you, Turk?" Hiney laughed.

"Thanks, Hiney," I said, giving him a slap on the back. "I owe you."

Lil' Mike ran back out to us and handed me a signed title to a 1968 Harley FLH. I held out the key to the trike for Lil' Mike.

"Go ahead. She's all yours!"

"Really, Turk? I can take this baby home?"

"Yeah, let's do this before I change my mind," I said, still pretending to be less than sure. "I'll get the title for you tomorrow."

"Hell yeah!" Lil' Mike yelled. "Just run me through the switches real quick, and I'm out of here."

"Sure, no problem."

None of the toggle switches were marked, so I went through each one of their functions. Lil' Mike kicked her to life, and I watched him play with the jockey shift.

"It's going to take some getting used to," I said. "Remember, it's a three-speed with a reverse."

Lil' Mike just nodded and with a smile, pulled the shifter back. After letting out a loud clunk, she was in first gear. Hiney and I watched the old '51 Panhead Trike roll off the lot and down the street, out of sight.

I was like a kid on Christmas morning with a new toy. "Let's go for a ride, Hiney!" I said. "Side-by-side this time."

Riding hard with the wind in my face and pipes screaming in my ears is what I lived for. Harleys were fun to ride and fun to work on. I could sit for hours in my garage tinkering with my bike. I loved making custom parts for it. Harleys have a mystique that only their owners can feel and understand.

When I was a teenager, a buddy of mine let me ride his '62 Sportster, and the rest was history. In my teens, I had ridden my share of Hondas,

Yamahas, and BSAs, but they didn't leave me with the feeling I got on that Harley. Not everyone gets the Harley bug, and that's good. Harley riders are a breed all their own. It's not that one bike is better than the other, it's how that particular bike makes you feel.

I grew up loving to play with Harleys, so when Hiney asked me to help him rebuild the top end on his 1952 Panhead, I jumped right in, feet first. It sounded like a fun project, and I couldn't wait to get started.

It was early Friday evening when he rolled his '52 rigid framed Harley Panhead into my garage. Once the frame was balanced on a pile of blocks, the tear-down started. The gas and oil tanks, seat and battery were removed, and then it was time to attack the engine.

Hiney and I worked all weekend on the heart of his old iron horse. We drank and laughed for two days straight. Our friendship was as solid and tight as his mill was when we finished it. There's no better way to bond with someone than spending time with each other doing something you both love.

Late Sunday night, we took her off the blocks and Hiney primed the engine with a couple of kicks with the switch off. Hiney looked at me for a moment. Then, with a shit-eating grin, he jumped up into the air and came down hard on the pedal, sending it to the floor with all his weight… nothing!

"Wait, Hiney! Did you turn the gas on?"

"Yeah, yeah, I did. I think."

He looked at the petcock, and it was on. He looked up at me and smiled. He knew he would have looked stupid if it had been off. I don't think there is a rider out there who hasn't done something stupid with his bike. I think I've done them all. Let's start with not turning the gas on or kicking her while still in gear. How about taking off with the kickstand down or having the bike fall over when you thought the kickstand was down. Been there done that.

Hiney primed her two more times, then turned the switch on again. He advanced the distributor, then kicked her again. He got a loud pop and a puff from the carb.

"Well, she's getting spark," Hiney said.

"Come on, Hiney," I laughed. "You're acting like you're afraid to start her. Kick the bitch!"

"Shut up, Turk! She might hear you!"

I stepped back and pulled my ass up onto the workbench. I popped a cold beer from the cooler next to me and chugged half of it. I pulled a second ice-cold beer out and held it up for Hiney to see.

"You don't get this until she starts," I said.

Hiney pumped the pedal a few more times, then stiff-legged it to the floor.

She fired loudly and came to life. Hiney reached down and adjusted the distributor and throttled her a few times. He sat there a minute and just listened to the engine idle with the straight pipes going *po-ta-to, po-ta-to, po-ta-to*.

I slid off the bench and tossed Hiney the beer.

"We did it, bro!" I yelled over the exhaust noise. "We brought her back to life. Time to break her in. What do you say we take a cruise around Red Rock Canyon?"

"I'm right behind you, man!"

As Hiney gazed at his puttering bike, he looked like he was staring into the face of his newborn child. Unless you've rebuilt your own engine, you can't understand the attachment a person has to something he has created. I watched him smile as the pipes called for the open road.

We rode through the canyon for a while at about 35 miles per hour to make sure everything seated properly. We stopped at Bonnie Springs and checked for leaks. It seemed that everything was holding up, so we made our way around the duck pond and into the bar for a couple cold ones.

While we sat and enjoyed our beers, Hiney opened up to me. He said he was going to leave the club and move back to Florida. He had a son there living with his ex-wife, and he felt it was time he became a part of his life. For a moment, I was upset to lose him, but I knew he was right. Family is important, and you must do what is right by them. The way I see it, women come and go in your life but your children are sacred.

I do love women, I just don't trust them. I had put my trust into the club and my bros. Now I was losing a bro, and it didn't sit right with me. But a man must do what he thinks is best for his children.

"Hiney, I wish you all the luck in the world on getting your family back together," I said, raising my glass to him.

"Thanks, Turk. That means a lot coming from you," he replied, touching his glass to mine.

About a month later, Hiney packed up his life and put Vegas in his rearview mirror. I missed having his over-friendly personality around, but he was home with his son and when I talked to him on the phone, he sounded happy. Even though I was happy for him, I knew I could never replace the friendship we had.

About a year after Hiney left, I was out with a couple of my bros riding down Nellis Boulevard when I saw a familiar place. The Cougars Den was the bar that Bill and I hung out at during our Fremont Street days. Gloria had been the cocktail waitress back then before I was in the club, and I wondered what ever happened to her. One day soon, I'm going to have to look her up.

I signaled for the guys to pull over, and we backed in by the front doors. I sat there a minute and remembered the last time I had left this bar. It was four years ago when I walked out these doors and kicked over my 1971 Harley XLCH Sportster for the last time. It was stolen that night.

I'd had a lot of great memories of this place, but I walked in and was immediately disappointed. It had been completely remodeled. There were pool tables where the dance floor used to be, and the lighting was much brighter.

Barflies need consistency in their lives. Bars that have not been remodeled seem to stay around for years. All the memories that have been created there by the customers are still alive. You feel comfortable in a bar that is home to your memories. The minute you remodel, it becomes a different place and your memories are torn down and thrown out with the scrap.

The Cougar's Den had become just another bar.

Booze was booze, so we had a round, but once we finished our drinks I was ready to head out. I ordered a round of shots for the road and handed them out to my bros.

"What are we toasting to, Turk?" Pegleg asked.

"Lost memories," I said. "They're gone, and so am I. Let's split."

We did our shots and slammed the glasses on the bar, bottoms up.

As I rose to leave, Grube yelled out, "Hey, Turk! How about one for the ditch?"

We all laughed and ordered another round of beer and shots. We ended up staying another hour or so just bullshitting. The old ones might be gone, but I guess new memories are always waiting to be made.

Once we were back on our bikes, we headed east toward Lake Mead and Boulder City. Lake Mead Boulevard connected Vegas with the lake by means of switchbacks and dips. The road could be treacherous if not navigated properly. This is where we came to test our riding skills. We rounded the bend coming over Sunrise Mountain and leaned hard to the right into the first turn.

If it hadn't been for the alcohol, we wouldn't have been so foolish.

Our bikes were not café racers and were definitely not set up for high-speed cornering, but we were young and invincible. It was the adrenaline rush we craved, and our chopped Harleys served it up.

Pegleg was in the lead with his Sportster and Grube behind him on his new Super Glide. I brought up the rear on my ol' shovelhead and did my best to keep up. I was no match for the lighter bikes with their narrow front ends. It didn't matter where you were in formation as long as you stayed on the road. We sped across the asphalt veins that stretched through the desert and soon saw Lake Mead in the distance.

The blue expanse of water looked out of place in the center of this lunar-like landscape that surrounded it. It looked so inviting that we increased our speed to hasten our arrival.

We made a left turn down a narrow asphalt single-lane road to the rocky beach. The lakefront was crowded with cars that had pulled right up to the water's edge. We found an open area to the far right and shut down our hot V-twin engines.

The sound of kids screaming and laughing filled the air. I walked to the edge, kicked off my boots, and stepped into the cool water.

"Hey Turk!" yelled Pegleg. "Aren't you going to take off your socks?"

"Naw, the damn rocks hurt my feet and anything over them helps."

I wanted to dive in, but cooling off from the knees down would have to do today. We had to get back on the road soon because we were meeting some guys at the bar in Boulder City.

I stood knee-deep in the lake and gazed at the families that lined the beach area. I watched as the adults played with their children, oblivious to the three of us standing on the beach. We might as well have been from another planet; their lives were so different from ours. They didn't even know that we existed unless they encountered us on the highways.

I watched a little girl run up and hug her daddy, and I thought of my daughter back in Virginia. I always felt an empty spot in my heart for her. Thinking of her always upset my stomach because I felt I needed to do more to see her. I didn't really know her, but that didn't mean I didn't miss her.

Suddenly, everything seemed to change. A strange sensation rushed through my body, warming my skin. I didn't know what was happening or how to explain it. I felt this numbness in my head like I had just arrived at this time and place. I had to force myself to remember how I had gotten here. Everything felt different and out of place. I could no longer hear the kids playing; the beach was quiet. I barely heard Grube talking to me.

"Hey Turk," Grube yelled, his voice slowly becoming clearer. "You all right? You look like you're in a daze."

"Yeah, I'm fine," I said as I leaned forward and splashed water on my face.

I thought maybe the hot air and the cold water were screwing with my mind. I waded through the water back to where my boots sat on the shoreline. I sat down and removed my socks to wring them out. After restoring my feet to a riding condition, I walked back up to my Harley. I could still hear the water squishing through my socks inside the boots.

I still had an annoying feeling that something was off. I didn't know what it was, but I figured that once I got back on the road, I'd be all right. As we pulled back out onto the highway, my mind flooded again with thoughts of my daughter. I don't know why, but I kind of wanted what Hiney had gone after in Florida.

Something inside me screamed that it was time for a change.

I loved to ride, and I knew that wouldn't change, but I wanted more. There was something missing in my life, and I needed to find out what it was.

We stopped in front of the bar in Boulder City and backed our bikes in. I stayed seated and watched Grube light a cigarette. Our two bros that had been waiting walked out to greet us.

We had announced to the club that we were riding out here today, but it was the five of us that showed.

"Turk!" Rotten Ralph yelled as he approached. "You need to call Baby Huey right now!"

"Why? What's up, Ralphie?" I didn't like the tone of his voice.

"All I can tell you is that it's bad, Turk. Real bad. Just call him."

I went inside and found the payphone between the restrooms. As I dialed the clubhouse number, I wondered what could be so wrong to have Ralph freaked out. After about ten long rings, Huey finally picked up the phone.

"Who's this?" Huey's voice grated.

"Wow, man. You sound like shit. It's Turk. What the hell is going on?"

"Turk…shit, man. I don't know how to say this, so I'm just going to spit it out," he said with a slight tremble in his voice. "We lost Hiney."

There was silence. "What do you mean 'lost.'"

Baron's mangled bike flashed in my mind, but I shoved it down, refusing to consider that.

"Turk…Hiney was killed in an accident when his bike collided with a truck last night. I'm sorry, man."

I couldn't answer. I got dizzy and weak in the knees. My throat felt like it was closing up and the phone receiver seemed to weigh 20 pounds in my hand. I almost dropped the phone as I fell against the wall. My mind flooded with thoughts of Hiney's face smiling as he rode next to me on his scoot.

I didn't know what to say as I slowly pulled the phone receiver back up to my ear. I felt something was wrong at the lake, but how could I have felt the news of Hiney's death?

"Huey," I forced out. "Huey, how…He was in Florida with his son. He was happy…Damn it! Sorry, Huey, I have to go." I was about to hang up when I heard him call out.

"Turk," he said as I returned the receiver to my ear. "Why don't you stop by the clubhouse, so we can talk."

"Thanks for letting me know, Huey. I'm just going to head home. I'll talk to you later."

I hung the phone up and held on to the receiver for a minute with my head against the wall. I felt like I needed to call someone, but I realized I had no one to call. My family was in Virginia, and all I had was the club out here, and the whole club had lost Hiney.

I knew it had been Hiney at the lake. Somehow he was telling me to get home and see my daughter because life is short.

When I walked outside, I saw that Rotten Ralph had already told the other guys. I guess Baby Huey wanted to tell me himself. All the guys walked over, and we had a group hug. There were reds eyes all around and a few silent tears. The air was completely still as we stood outside, holding each other that hot summer day—the day I lost my best friend.

"You know what, guys?" I said, clearing my throat. "I think I'm going to head on back to town."

"Come on, Turk," Pegleg said. "Let's go inside and have a shot. You know, pour one out for Hiney."

"I don't think so. Thanks anyway," I said. "I don't think a shot will settle right in my stomach right this moment. I'm just going to head home. I'll catch you guys later."

"You want us to ride with you?" Grube asked.

"No, I'm good, really. You guys go ahead and have a shot for Hiney. I'm out of here."

I started my bike and felt its weight as I pulled her up off the kickstand. I drove off leaving the guys in front of the bar, staring at me ride off. It was only 35 miles to my place in town, and I don't remember any of that ride. I was mentally and emotionally drained when I pulled into my garage. I hit the couch and lay there till I passed out.

When I woke up, a deep depression consumed my body. I didn't want to do anything. I was mad at the world and wanted to hit something, but I didn't have the strength to even make a fist. I kept picturing Hiney hitting that truck. I couldn't shake it.

I didn't move until late the next night when my body's survival mode kicked in, and I made myself get up and drink a beer with some chips. I didn't leave my house for two days.

As the weeks wore on, I tried to keep myself busy. I found a few things that helped to ease the feeling of something being missing in my life. It was as if my mind had opened to a whole new set of values. Life seemed so unpredictable now. I guess it was the whole here today, gone tomorrow kind of thing.

A buddy of mine from work told me that as a veteran, I could get paid by the government to go to college. Getting a nice check every month sounded good, so I enrolled for the fall semester.

While in my first year at college, I decided to try out for the baseball team. I made the grade and became the team's catcher. I was having a great time playing ball and meeting college girls.

Soon all my time was occupied. I was working full time as the valet manager at the Mint Hotel, going to college twice a week, and alternating days between baseball and karate classes. And, of course, I still attended club meetings and mandatory runs. I somehow managed to squeeze everything in, but had no time to spare. Even still, the feeling I'd gotten by Lake Mead had never really gone away.

I was so busy trying to find out who I was that I was actually missing out on what was most important in life. I soon realized that family was the answer. The club was my family here, but I had a daughter, and I needed to be a part of her life.

I was constantly talking about Hiney at the club meetings. I just couldn't accept the fact that he was gone. Being around the club didn't help me get over his death either.

After a while, I realized the guys would just ignore me when I mentioned him. They'd just say, "Yeah, we know Turk. We all miss him," and walk away. I let them all know in uncertain terms how much that pissed me off.

One Wednesday night, the club meeting was going along as usual when suddenly, I was done. I walked into the middle of the living room and pulled my vest off. I hadn't planned to do it, but I believe the desire to call it quits with the club had been quietly building in me since Hiney's death. He'd brought me into the club, and now, with his passing, my time to leave had come too. My journey with the club had run its course, and it was time to move on.

"This club was about honor and dignity. It was about loyalty and brotherhood, but I haven't felt any of that since Hiney's death."

"What the hell are you talking about, Turk?" Doc shouted. "We all loved Hiney, and it's a sad thing he's gone, but we have to get on with our lives."

"You're right. We do," I said. "And that's exactly what I plan to do." I placed my colors on the table in front of Doc.

He stared at the vest silently for a moment, then said calmly, "Turk, you're the last person I thought would quit this club."

"Yeah, me too," I said. "I might be making a big mistake, but it's something I have to do right now."

Everyone was still. After a minute or two, Baby Huey grabbed my vest and pulled out his knife. It's club policy to cut the patches off the vest belonging to any member who leaves. Huey put his knife to my vest but hesitated.

"There's not a knife in the world sharp enough to cut the patches off this man's vest," Huey said pointing at me and returning his knife to his sheath.

"Turk, you're under a lot of stress right now," Doc said gently. "You're being a little irrational. I'm going to hang on to your vest. The door will always be open for you if you ever decide to come back."

I smiled. "Thanks Doc, that means a lot. I'm not sure where my head is at right now, but I need to step back and figure out where I'm headed in my life. I know I don't have the answers you want to hear about why I'm leaving. Hell, it's a mystery to me. I love the club, but I have to find what's missing."

"You're a good bro, Turk," Doc said, slapping me on the back. "A major pain in the ass, but that's another story. Take care of yourself, brother."

"I'm not going to disappear, I'll be around."

Everyone stood up and hugged me and wished me luck as I walked towards the door. As I drove away from the clubhouse, I almost regretted my decision, but I kept riding. I had been so focused on retribution for so long that once it was gone, it didn't take long to notice that it hadn't been what I'd been craving all along. I still didn't know what it was I needed, but I was excited to be free to find out.

I rode home without a patch on my back for the first time in four years. To my surprise I had actually enjoyed the ride home after quitting the club. I didn't have to look over my shoulder for the cops or other clubs gunning for me.

I was just another civilian...and for once it felt good.

EPILOGUE

Three years later, I graduated from Clark County Community College with two degrees—an AA in Applied Science and an AAS in Hotel Technology. College was a fun experience for me, and it took me to a whole new level in life. It gave me the knowledge and confidence I needed to tackle any job I wanted.

I continued my martial arts training for almost 20 years. I now hold a Black Belt in Tae Kwon Do and a fourth degree Black Belt in Kobayashi Okinawan Shorin Ryu. I want to also mention that I met three of my lifelong friends in the dojo—Tony Gamboa, Miguel Hierro, and Mark Hodsdon.

I am also a PADI Five-Star Certified Advanced Open Water Diver. Scuba diving opened my eyes to a whole other world that lay just beneath the surface of the ocean. When you're 80 feet below the surface, you might as well be in outer space. You have to learn to deal with atmospheric pressure changes, decompression requirements, and buoyancy issues, not to mention the chance of being attacked by a creature you usually find in a sushi bar.

As I look back on my life, it seems like I had to change my career every 10 years or so. I started in Vegas as a valet attendant and became the manager of day shift from 1971 till 1979. Then I moved inside as a bellman from 1979 to 1990. After that, I ventured into the trade I loved the most; I became a bartender in local clubs for over 14 years (my first book, *Lines on the Bar… Whiskey on the Rocks* is about my life as a bartender in Sin City). I now work at a major hotel on the strip, and it has been a great journey.

My family is the best a man could ask for. My children are Wendy, Brent, Darret, Kymmy, and Jessica. I have 12 grandchildren, and three great-grandchildren, and, of course, my dog Boo.

I've been single for many years now, which gives me plenty of time to ride my Harley.

1971—Harley "Stolen Steel" Sportster

1974—Stroker

1975—Baron and Rotten Ralph

1975—Nevada Highway Patrol always checking on us

Lance, Peggy, and Baby Huey

1976—Las Vegas County Cops

1976—Another NHP stop with Pegleg, Baron, Dude, and Norton

1975—Las Vegas Autorama Show

Hiney's Panhead before the rebuild

Hiney's Panhead after the rebuild

1974—My 1968 Harley Shovelhead

1974—Las Vegas Autorama Show

The Piece of Ass Raffle

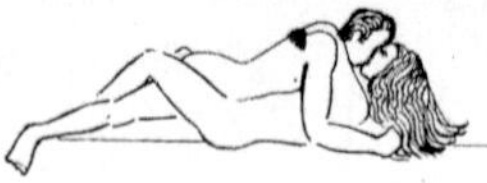

First Annual
N.M.C.
Piece of Ass Drawing
All-Expense Paid Trip to Lathrop Wells
or
$100.00 Cash
Drawing February 2, 1976, 1:00 p.m.
At Custom Cycle Accessories
2960 Westwood Drive, Unit 21
DONATION $1.00

№ 625

Name
Add.
Phone
№ 625

ABOUT THE AUTHOR

Rick Hart moved to Las Vegas from Virginia in 1969 while in the U.S. Air Force. After leaving the military, Rick attained a Fourth Degree Black Belt in Shorin Ryu Karate and became a Five Star PADI Scuba Diver. Rick also received two degrees from the Clark County Community College and now works at a major resort hotel on the Las Vegas Strip. Rick loves spending time with his five kids, 12 grandkids, three great-grandchildren, and his Boo-Doggy. He enjoys riding his Harley as much as always through the mountains that surround the Las Vegas valley.